FLY
CHA

Also by Caroline Akrill
non-fiction
NOT QUITE A HORSEWOMAN
fiction
EVENTER'S DREAM
A HOOF IN THE DOOR
TICKET TO RIDE

FLYING CHANGES

Caroline Akrill

J. A. ALLEN
London

FLYING CHANGES
*first published 1985 by
Arlington Books (Publishers) Ltd
15–17 King Street, St. James's
London S.W.1*

Allen Equestrian Fiction paperback edition 1989

© *Caroline Akrill 1985*

*Typeset by Inforum Ltd, Portsmouth
Printed and bound in Great Britain by
Biddles Ltd, Guildford and King's Lynn*

British Library Cataloguing in Publication Data

*Akrill, Caroline
Flying changes.
I. Title
823'.914[F]*

ISBN 0-85131-493-7

For my mother and father with love

DISCLAIMER

The author would like to stress that no character in this book relates to any person living or dead and that all incidents are entirely imaginary.

ACKNOWLEDGEMENTS

Jennie Loriston-Clarke for the loan of DUTCH COURAGE for the book jacket, Peter Egan for giving Oliver substance, Charles Harris for help with dressage technicalities, Elaine How for artistic endeavour beyond the call of duty.

ONE

Oliver was livid when he found out. John Englehart had warned that he would be, but still it took me by surprise. What made matters worse was that I didn't even tell him properly, it just slipped out by accident.

He had just finished one of his celebrated exhibitions and he came into the commentary box in his tail coat with the doeskin waistcoat and the suede-seated white breeches.

"Make a note, Kathryn," he said in his precise way, "that next time I would like the music switched after the flying changes and before the *passage*; the tempo of the second piece is more suited to collected movements."

He looked, as ever, incredibly cool and elegant. The only sign that he had performed for two solid hours on four different horses were the sweat clouds on the inside of his boots and the rein-welts across the fingers of his white kid gloves. Experts maintain that only the supremely confident can afford to wear white gloves for dressage, but naturally, Oliver always had the most perfect hands.

I had lodged in my mind at that particular moment an irritant of a different nature, concerning the non-appearance of the Swedish Decanters. These graceful objects had been delivered earlier in the day, each one enclosed in polystyrene and crated against the journey, and as Oliver had done the choosing they were in the very best of taste; a perfectly plain claret shape in heavy glass with a bubble suspended in the base and a matching bubble stopper. The trouble with the bubble stoppers had been that they refused to budge, and when I had tried to loosen the wax seal under the tap, the water had been unexpectedly hot and the first decanter had divided neatly into two halves. So now, with *Question Time* imminent, and Oliver confidently expecting the sponsor's obligatory sherry to be dispensed from the decanter instead of the bottle – he strove hard against the stigma of commercialism, even though the place was owned, down to the stable staff anoraks and the paper napkins, by *Tio Fino* – the Swedish Decanters were still lying in their polystyrene shrouds with their bubble stoppers stuck fast, and one of them was broken.

Preoccupied with this discomforting knowledge, I pushed the demonstration folder (in the inevitable *Tio Fino* beige with the blue and ruby border and the discreet trademark of an Andalusian horse) over to John Englehart, who was gathering together his commentary notes in the nervous fluster Oliver's presence inevitably induced in him, and asked him to make the alteration.

"Because next time," I countered, as he raised his brown, spaniel eyes in reproach and shuffled anew to locate a pen, "I won't be here, if you remember."

Within the few seconds of silence which followed upon this ill-considered announcement, the unfortunate John Englehart, knowing himself revealed as an accessory, appeared to be affected by paralysis, the pen transfixed above the page, whilst I, the decanters forgotten in the face of this new dilemma, stared at Oliver, holding my breath, praying that he hadn't heard; that by a miracle, the significance of my indiscretion had somehow escaped him. It had not.

Oliver just stood, and after the briefest flash of incredulity, his eyes froze into chips of ice. "And where will you be Kathryn," he enquired in a smooth and interested voice, "when you are not here to remind Mr. Englehart to change the music?"

I didn't know what to say. The tactful presentation of unwelcome news has never been my forte, and if I have ever achieved it, it has not been without a good deal of agonised rehearsal. Now, totally unprepared, I faced the most convoluted rendition of my life.

"Well, Kathryn?"

I could have lied, I suppose. It would have been the easiest thing to have invented a dental appointment, or an unexpected invitation with which to explain my absence on the day of the next demonstration and Oliver would have believed it – why wouldn't he? And it would have been simple after that, to pack my belongings and steal away, leaving a brief note containing a partial explanation for my departure. In the circumstances, it might have been the most sensible way, but:

"I won't be here, Oliver," I said, "because I am about to give you notice. I'm leaving." I was surprised to hear how matter-of-fact it sounded.

Oliver didn't look surprised. He was too well disciplined now to show emotion. It seemed to me that the discipline of his art had taken over his life, and that his art had filled his life to the exclusion of everything and everyone not connected with it. Even so, something about the way he looked caused a little knot of emotion to unravel itself in a wholly unwelcome and frightening manner inside my chest. I knew that it was neither the time nor the place for explanations, but I could not be silent.

"I can't stay, Oliver," I said, "because if I do I shall probably go mad. I just can't cope. The atmosphere is beginning to affect my nerves. I'm beginning to mislay things. I forget things. I even break things. . ." Already my voice had taken on a hysterical note as I prepared to confess to breaking the decanter, but John Englehart, revived by the possibility of an unpleasant scene in which he might be called upon to take my side against his employer, towards whom his feelings veered hourly between dog-like devotion and vicious resentment, applied a sharp elbow to my ribs.

"Not *now* Kathryn," he said in a scandalised voice, "you can't possibly go into all that now, not when people are waiting, there isn't *time* ."

Oliver's face was glacial. And, of course, there wasn't time. He knew perfectly well that his audience would be waiting: the BHS students nursing their carefully prepared questions about *renvers* and *travers*; the professional instructors and judges, looking to analyse, longing to criticise, seeking to fault his performance even when no fault could be found, hoping in their secret hearts that this time they would find him less perfect that the last. There would be the handful of international experts, secure enough in their own position to be fulsome about the suspended elevation of the *passage*, the rhythmic spring of the *piaffe*, the perfectly cadenced bound of the *pirouette*. And there were the ladies, always for Oliver, the ladies; the young and the not-so-young, waiting their opportunity to speak to him, to be charmed by him, to stand close to him, to touch him, to ask for autographs, photographs. Because at twenty-seven years of age, my brother, Oliver Jasny, was the darling of the dressage set; the fêted, talented, stunningly aristocratic exponent of *haute école*.

It was at this point that one of the caballerizos (the Spanish grooms) who had been hovering in an agony of uncertainty outside the partition, in all probability despatched to remind Oliver that his presence was not only passionately desired, but paid for in advance, managed to summon enough courage to tap upon the glass to gain his attention. Oliver, whose only perceptible movement so far had been a tightening of the jaw, shot him a glance savage enough to send him scuttling away down the gallery steps. Then, in a deliberately controlled gesture, he pulled off his gloves one finger at a time and dropped them singly onto the demonstration folder.

I might have imagined that only I knew how angry he was, but I noticed John Englehart flinch and I looked at his agonised face and resolved that I, at least should not be intimidated. And so I was able to meet his icy gaze in a resolute, if not entirely dispassionate manner, but even so, I was not unaffected by that marvellously beautiful face. It sounds extreme I know, when used to describe a man, but beautiful was the only way to describe it; the fine regularity of the features, the fair, golden hair, straight and swept above the dark curve of the eyebrow, the thick-lashed glamour of the brilliantly contemptuous blue eyes, the sensual mouth.

But now, the sensual mouth was clamped into an uncompromisingly tight line, and the brilliant blue eyes were like flint, and as the door of the insubstantial commentary box slammed against his abrupt departure and the entire structure quivered, John Englehart lunged forward not quite in time to prevent his commentary notes from the slipping off the table.

"I *told* you he'd be a bitch about it," he said.

TWO

"Sherry, Kathryn?" Oliver raised an enquiring eyebrow over his own particular blend of super-dry fino.

"Why not?" I sat on the edge of a wing chair wanting nothing but to have the whole thing over with. How odd life is, I thought, when hundreds of people, thousands, would give anything to be in Oliver Jasny's private sitting room and just at this moment, I would give anything, everything, to be somewhere else.

Oliver poured a second glass and handed it to me without comment. He knew I hated it. He walked slowly over to the french windows and stared out in the direction of the stables. He never drew the curtains. It didn't seem to occur to him that someone, unknown and unseen in the darkness, might be out there, watching him. That, lit from within like an actor on stage set, he was exposed and vulnerable in his own home. Or perhaps it did occur to him and he was indifferent to it.

I was not going to speak first. I turned the glass of pale, undrinkable liquid in my hands, and my eyes wandered restlessly around the room. It was furnished sparsely and with typical refinement; two wing chairs, a pembroke table to hold the drinks, a knowle settee. Touches of the sponsors were evident in the long coffee table with the tooled Spanish leather top, and the branched wrought-iron lamp. There were no ornaments, no photographs, nothing personal, only a John Skeaping bronze on the mantle shelf, and above it, a water-colour of Oliver riding San Domingo, his best and most famous horse. It was a masterly portrait, painted by a leading artist, displaying all the power and brilliance of the magnificent Andalusian, but it was not a picture to delight a dressage enthusiast. The bay coat was flecked with foam, the neck overbent, the mane unplaited. There was a wildness about the horse wholly inappropriate to the art of dressage, and yet in comparison, Oliver's self-discipline was complete as, hatless and unsmiling, he controlled the horse with the lightest touch on the rein. If the painter had exercised artistic licence in his portrayal of San Domingo, he had clearly been under severe restraint when it came to his rider. Oliver's elegance, his effortless style, his chilling disdain had been captured to perfection, but there was not a hint, not the slightest glimpse of the person underneath. It had occurred to me more than once during the last two months that there might no longer be a person underneath; that the Oliver I had worshipped all through my childhood had gone forever. But common sense told me that this could not be so, and I still believed that somewhere beneath the seemingly impermeable shell of condescension and indifference with which he surrounded himself, I would find the Oliver I had once known, the Oliver who had once loved and needed me, and perhaps still did. I turned away from the picture. I took a tentative sip of the super-dry fino. I thought it might descale a bathtub very nicely.

"Kathryn," Oliver said, "this evening was terrible."
"Yes," I agreed. "I know."
"Where were the decanters?"
"I couldn't get the stoppers out," I said, "and then I broke one."
"You broke one." He was wearing silver-grey corduroy trousers with a black silk shirt open at the neck to show a thick chain of Spanish silver. He did not turn towards me as he spoke. His voice was as dry as his sherry.
"It was an accident, Oliver. I tried to free the stopper under the hot tap and the whole thing cracked in half."
"You could have read the instructions. They were perfectly clear. You soak out the stoppers in warm water to which you have added . . ."
". . . a little detergent. I know. I found the instructions later, they were in the bottom of the crate, under the decanters; by that time it was too late." It was galling to realise that he had checked, that he already knew.
"And the books, Kathryn. What happened to the books?"
I sighed. In my anxiety over the decanters I had omitted to put out the books. We usually sold at least two dozen copies of *Oliver Jasny's Dressage* after each demonstration. This time there was no excuse to be made and I made none.
"And the videos?"
My heart dropped. I had not even remembered that I had forgotten the videos, and whilst I had decided to put forward my inefficiency as one of the chief reasons for my departure, I had not envisaged being made to feel I might be understating my case.

"Oliver," I said, "all this proves that it was a mistake for me to come here. I shall never be any use to you in an administrative capacity because I am not suited to the work, you must see that."

There was a pause whilst Oliver walked back to the sherry and refilled his glass. This time he did not invite me to join him. "All I can see, Kathryn," he said with asperity, "is that you appear to lack application. It is only a matter of organisation. I do not ask you to do a lot – the work is not difficult."

I looked down into my glass, knowing just how difficult it had been, but also knowing that if I considered the duties which comprised my organisation of Oliver's working day, I would be forced to agree with him, because the work was not difficult. In the morning I sorted his mail, paid his bills, sent out signed photographs, set aside his personal correspondence, attended to the filing. I then had to select two classical tape cassettes and deliver them to John Englehart in the commentary box. Oliver's class of promising riders, each individually auditioned and selected for training by the Dressage Improvement Board, would already be assembling below in the Olympic sized arena with its vast mirrors and polished kicking boards, and it was John Englehart's task to welcome them, to oversee their riding-in, and to prepare them for Oliver. The riding-in and part of the instruction was given to a background of music as an aid to fluency and relaxation. On the previous day to the accompaniment of Beethoven's Ninth Symphony, Oliver had made his entrance, bareheaded and on foot, in cream breeches and brown boots, his open-collared shirt topped with a leather gilet, just as one of his protégés had been soundly deposited upon the tan by a particularly mischievous fly-buck. Casually he had stretched out an arm and taking the rein of the horse as it cantered past him, had arrested its flight and returned it to its rider, whom, with the politest of attention, he assisted back into the saddle before turning to greet the class as a whole. As an entrance, as a piece of timing, it had been magnificent, and yet there had been nothing contrived about it, nothing planned.

"Sometimes," John Englehart had said in a constricted voice, "it makes me sick just to watch him."

After the class I collected the fees; thirty pounds from each pupil and not a penny of it subsidized by the Dressage Board. It was considered an honour to be chosen, a privilege to pay, and no one ever intimated that it might be excessive. Naturally, Oliver was never seen to handle money or to indulge in small-talk after the class. It hardly mattered. The elevating combination of Beethoven and Oliver Jasny had such an intoxicating effect that the pupils emerged from the indoor school emotionally shattered, coiling gamgee and bandages with unsteady fingers, leading their expensive horses up the ramps in a euphoric daze, clipping the gateposts with their Range Rovers and trailers as they drove away. The rest of my day was spent either on the telephone, in liaison with the sponsors over expenses, publicity, arrangements for demonstrations, teach-ins, and the touring dressage clinic, or at the typewriter, answering general correspondence, fending off social invitations which rained in for Oliver in a never-ending stream and were never, under any circumstances, accepted, in making out stable duty lists for the caballerizos, in preparing commentary notes for John Englehart.

"No," I admitted finally, "it isn't difficult."

"Oh," Oliver turned at last, affecting mock surprise. "You agree?"

I felt the first stirrings of exasperation. "Well of course I agree. It couldn't be described as a difficult job. Almost anyone could do it."

Oliver sat down on the other wing chair and stared at me. "But Kathryn," he said in a perplexed tone, "you do not seem able to do it."

His formal manner, the stilted language he used, the way he chose to ignore the fact that I was his sister, speaking to me as if I was just a recalcitrant employee, infuriated me. And yet I had resolved not to lose my temper. I did not want things to end badly between us.

"It isn't that I *can't* do it," I explained, "only that I don't have an aptitude for it – typing, filing, office duties, have never appealed to me. I find it hard to apply myself. I lose concentration." I wondered why it should be necessary to explain how I felt when once there had been no need of explanations, when once a glance would have told us all we needed to know. "Any job is made easier," I said peevishly, "if the work is enjoyable."

"You knew, Kathryn, when you came here, that I could only offer you a position as my personal assistant," Oliver said sharply.

I said nothing. What was there to say? Of course I had known it, but the truth was that I would have accepted any job, I would have washed the windows, swept the floors, I would have cleaned out the drains if that was what I had to do to be reunited with Oliver.

"I told you exactly what your duties would be. I explained most carefully."

This was also true. But other, more important things had not been explained. Four years of discipline in the dressage schools of Europe had turned my brother into a stranger who intimidated and terrified everyone who worked under him, and yet this same cold, elegant stranger was himself stage-managed from above by the omnipresent, omnipotent hand of the sponsor, and moved in such an atmosphere of highly-charged tension that the very air around him seemed charged with a feverish emotion. I had seen my brother in many compromising situations before, and all of his own choosing, but never one as potentially unhealthy as this.

"I think we should both admit that it was a mistake for me to come here," I said. "I should have known that I would never enjoy secretarial work. I should have realised I would never be happy working away from the horses."

Oliver frowned. "It is impossible for me to offer you a position with the horses, Kathryn, you know that."

"I wouldn't dream of asking you to. Everyone knows you never employ female labour in the yards." I was unable to keep the edge out of my voice.

"I was not responsible for that decision," he replied in an even tone, "*Tio Fino* made the rule."

Yes, I thought, but you agreed to it, but then you would, wouldn't you Oliver? I did not actually trust myself to speak. I was too chilled by the proximity of thin ice to open my mouth.

"If you are thinking of going back to work for Francesca," Oliver said, "I am sure you will have considered the substantial drop in salary."

"Money isn't all that important to me." I looked at him

in irritation. It was disturbing and somehow even shaming to realise he still knew me well enough to guess what my plans were when I no longer knew him at all.

". . . I believe it is something of an understatement to say that the accommodation is abysmal . . ."

I thought of the accommodation, the delapidated cottage with its sweating floors, its black beetles, its rotting soleplate, its damp-mottled walls. I gritted my teeth.

". . . the absence of an indoor manège means you will have to work outdoors even in the most disagreeable weather . . ."

"Do you think I don't know it?" I snapped. I was trying to stay calm, but already my palms were damp and I could feel my heart speeding ominously in my chest. He was speaking to me as if I was an imbecile and totally incapable of giving any consideration to what was involved.

". . . the hours will be endlessly inconvenient, and Francesca – well . . ." He leaned back in the chair and surveyed me in a cool and slightly amused manner as he evaluated Francesca, "Francesca is not always . . . congenial."

Congenial! I wanted to shout: Who the hell are the congenial people here, Oliver? You, who barely allow yourself to acknowledge that I exist? John Englehart, who can't wait to see the back of me so that he can make himself even more indispensable to you? Or the caballerizos, so much in awe of you that they tremble at your approach, and so jealous of their charges that even to reach out a hand towards a silky, Andalusian neck is to invite a hostile glance. Congenial, I could have shouted, don't make me laugh, Oliver! But instead, by a super-human effort of self-control, I managed to stay silent. I did not look at him. I kept my eyes on my glass. At times like this, I thought, it must be very soothing to be able to reach for a cigarette, but I had never smoked.

We sat in silence for a while, my brother and I, the one coolly watchful, the other trembling with suppressed fury and trying not to show it.

"Of course," Oliver said eventually, "there is a possibility that we could agree to a compromise."

"A compromise?" I had not expected this. I looked up. "What kind of compromise?"

"If you would agree to stay, I could speak to *Tio Fino*. There is a possibility that I could persuade them to allocate you a horse."

"Allocate me a *horse?*" I stared at him stupidly.

"But why not? You have the experience. You trained, as I did, with Count Von Der Drehler, and you are perfectly capable of teaching dressage at the basic level. I need a second rider, and if *Tio Fino* approved your change of status you need no longer concern yourself with office duties, you could work with me." And because I continued to stare at him dumbly, he added, "That is what you wanted, is it not?"

"Is it?" I managed to say.

"I rather thought so." The golden head was resting on the back of the chair, and one eyebrow was raised in an enquiring manner. "Well Kathryn, what do you think?"

"What do I think?" I looked across at him and the thick-lashed blue eyes looked back at me steadily. I thought him shameless and heartless and very, very beautiful. "I think you are a swine, Oliver," I said, "I think you had this in mind all the time, I think you could have done it from the beginning, but you chose not to."

Abruptly, the glass which had been twirling idly in the talented fingers stopped twirling.

"I think you brought me here to teach me a lesson, to punish me for choosing to stay with Francesca instead of following you to Europe five years ago. I think you deliberately set out to demonstrate your indifference to me and, if I think correctly, you have succeeded better than you know."

Oliver's expression did not change. Only his eyes gave an indication of the lowering temperature.

"I also think," I continued somewhat shakily as I struggled, and failed to disguise my anger, "that you don't believe I really want to leave at all, you think I would actually prefer to stay. I think you consider me as much in thrall as the rest of your sycophantic followers, ready to fly to your side at the lifting of an eyebrow, at the raising of your little finger."

"And am I wrong in that assumption?"

"You are," I said. "I have been your alter ego, your underling all my life, Oliver, but this is the end of all that. You will not persuade me to stay by any means."

"I see." Oliver got up from his chair. He seemed untouched by the anger in my voice. He walked over to the pembroke table and replaced the glass upon the silver tray.

I got up to leave. In retrospect, it would have been wiser not to have said any more, but I was enraged by his attitude, by the way he had ignored and humiliated me, by the way he had offered me the opportunity to become second rider only now, when I had thought to leave him, and by the way he had taken my compliance completely for granted.

"You still don't believe I'll go, do you," I demanded. "I wonder why that is? Is it because you think I can't live without you? Or is it because you think this place is so marvellous so fantastic, that nobody of sound mind would ever want to work anywhere else? Is that it?"

The criticism inherent in the latter question appeared to have some effect. Oliver turned. "I would have imagined that working for me would have been vastly preferable to working for Francesca," he said in a cold voice.

Somehow this reference to Francesca was the last straw and all of my earnest desire to say nothing I might later regret was forgotten.

"My God, but you're an arrogant snob, Oliver," I cried, "as well as a manipulated fool! Do you really think I have enjoyed working here? Can't you see what a precariously artifical set-up it is? Don't you realise that you're being stage-managed every step of the way? Would you really like to know what I think of your bloody precious dressage horses, your frightened little caballerizos, your bloody mixed-up sidekick, John Englehart? Shall I tell you Oliver? Shall I?" I was about to tell him anyway, because I could not stop myself. "Don't you care that you are being exploited?" I raged at him, "Don't you realise that it isn't art any longer, but show-business that you are into? Don't you know that you are being packaged like a detergent, marketed, hyped by your sponsors for commercial gain? Can't you see that when they have capitalised on your talent and exhausted your popularity, they will dump you out with the garbage without a second thought . . ." The expression of controlled fury on his face prevented me, warned me, not to go on. I tailed off. Already my own anger had evaporated. Already I was appalled.

"Oliver," I said desperately, "I didn't mean it. You know what I'm like; that somehow, I always manage to say the wrong thing . . ."

He did not look at me. He did not speak.

"I was angry . . .you made me angry . . .you made me say it . . ."

He walked over to the door. He opened it.

"Oliver," I pleaded, "Oliver, *please* . . ."

He held open the door and stood, waiting for me to leave. Only a few feet of carpet separated us, but it might as well have been a continent. I knew I would never reach him now, never. There was no way I could retract what I had said, and why should there be? Who was I to criticise when I had never achieved anything noteworthy in my life, and anyway, what was wrong with commercialism in a commercial age? How else could Oliver have achieved all this by the age of twenty-seven without sponsorship, and what sponsors would have backed him if he had not had magic? Magic, talent, ambition, dedication and glamour. There was never any doubt, especially in my own mind, and even at that very moment, that my brother had all these attributes, and more.

I thought it best to leave. On my way out I tried once more to apologise but was silenced by a dismissive wave of his hand. Once again he was elegantly composed, the impeccable facade was intact. The damage, if there had been any, had been swiftly repaired, the blue eyes were disinterested, the sensual mouth disdainful. His manner was as one who had been slightly inconvenienced by an unexpected visitor whose departure must be hastened without any obvious lapse of good manners. It was as if my outburst had never occurred. As if I had dreamed it.

Grabbing the outside handle, I slammed the door for all I was worth.

THREE

"If we take a leading rein each, and sandwich the rest of the little blighters between us, we might just get them all back alive," Francesca said in a grim voice.

We stood in the stable yard surrounded by a mêlée of ponies and children and fretting parents. For once, it wasn't actually raining, but the air was unwholesomely cold and damp, beading every possible surface with moisture and making me wish I had worn something more waterproof than a jersey.

"I suppose it *is* inevitable they go out on another hack," a parent enquired, "Davina *much* prefers a formal lesson, and she did say she received very little personal attention last week. It isn't that one doesn't comprehend the problem, but one is *paying* for instruction, after all."

There were many suitable replies I could have made to this: that the black ash manège had been entirely swallowed by the mud; that it was unrealistic to expect personal attention on a hack when there were so many novice riders to supervise; that riding out was in itself a form of instruction, instilling road sense and country lore, encouraging observation and independence, and that many children, Davina excluded, preferred it. However, two weeks at Pond Cottage Riding School had convinced me that the paying client was God and instead I heard myself promising to make the child my own personal responsibility.

I helped shivering children into damp saddles, tucked slimy leather into keepers, tweaked up girths, adjusted hat-straps more firmly under infant chins, altered stirrup leathers, clipped a leading rein onto a fat piebald and mounted a roan with long, white stockings and a blaze which ended in a pink, vulnerable nose. I wondered if riding school work quite suited me.

Francesca, mounted on an excitable chestnut, rode towards the gate with her beginner in tow, calling the ride into some semblance of order behind her. Her jodhpurs were ingrained with dirt, her anorak torn, her boots smeared and caked with mud. Her hair was twisted into a ragged pigtail, her cheeks were chapped, her lips flaking, and the classically perfect nose which lifted her looks above the merely pretty, was red at the tip from exposure. In marked contrast, the chestnut's coat gleamed, its mane was neatly laid, its tail immaculately pulled at the dock and trimmed below the hocks. I had long ceased to ponder the logic of Francesca's priorities. The morning after I had arrived I had appeared in the yard wearing jeans, and Francesca had been shocked. "I *never* wear jeans," she had said, "I like to look professional. We must keep up appearances." It had been on the tip of my tongue to point out that appearances might be better maintained in clean jeans than in jodhpurs that no amount of washing could restore to their original colour, but previous indiscretions had left their mark, and I said nothing. Since than I had worn jodhpurs as well, but mine were brown, as a defence against the sweat, the horse hairs, the glycerine saddle soap, the mucking out, and the appallingly insidious mud.

I took up my position at the rear of the ride with the fat piebald at my side and Davina, a thin, grave child mounted on a placid dun, in front. The hooves of our cavalcade clattered cheerfully along the lane which bordered Francesca's land, but the view from the saddle was far from cheerful. Beyond the scrappy, wire-reinforced hedge the mud of the manège was hock deep. Alongside lay the flooded jumping paddock with its scattering of rusted oil drums, its listing wings, its stacked banks of tyres; and as if this were not depressing enough, on either side of us stretched the poached, impoverished acres of grazing where the gateways were impassable and where no blade of grass showed. I wondered if Francesca, when she had made the decision to start her own business from scratch, starting at the bottom, catering for children and beginner riders at grass-root level, had realised that the bottom would be quite so low-lying, and that the grass roots, if there were any, would be drowning.

At the head of the procession Francesca struck out at a steady trot, setting the uneven line of velvet caps bobbing. Beyond the roan cob's pricked ears, Davina rose up and down, stiff-backed, her fingers too tight upon the reins, and, level with my stirrup, a chubby infant bumped happily in the saddle with the frighteningly loose innocence of the very young, lurching forward in a heart-stopping manner in order to pat the fat piebald on its damp neck and giving me the benefit of a radiant smile. I was greatly troubled by responsibility.

Pond Cottage Riding School, as I saw it, had two

serious deficiencies. The first was lack of capital, and the second as a direct result of the first, was lack of land. The cottage, its buildings and its six waterlogged acres belonged to a local speculative builder who had bought it in the hope that he might eventually be granted planning permission, but the council had so far proved intractable, and Francesca had now been in residence for five years. The fact that her position was precarious, that the council might one day recant, rendering her stable of twenty equines homeless, was something Francesca didn't allow herself to think about.

"Why worry myself hairless over something which may never happen?" she had said when I mentioned it, "Why cross bridges before I come to them?"

"Why bury your head in the sand? Why not face facts and be prepared?" I might have replied – but didn't.

In common with many small riding schools in green-belt areas, Francesca's establishment was welcomed by those who patronised it, and loathed by local residents who liked their countryside tidy and picturesque. Thus they complained to the council that she made use of the footpaths where they exercised their dogs and demanded that stiles be erected to prevent equine access. They despatched a spokesman to demand that she remove her manure bags from the side of the lane where they had been displayed for sale, the better to catch the eye of passing motorists. Even the wide, laneside verges, previously utilised as a refuge from speeding traffic and to save shod steel, now carried council-erected signs which proclaimed NO HORSE RIDING.

Francesca also waged a fierce battle against a local farmer who periodically tried to discourage her from exercising her legal right to use a bridleway which crossed his land by blocking the ride with heavy farm machinery, ploughing right up to the headlands, and padlocking the gates on the pretext that people had been letting his cattle out. Such concentrated opposition might have disheartened others, but not Francesca who, her brows knitted with annoyance over her grey-green eyes, wrote letters of complaint to the council and the British Horse Society Bridleways Officer, resulting in the eventual removal of the machinery, the flattening of the headland, the unpadlocking of the gates. Now, her face set, she reined in the chestnut at the head of the ride and stared down at two bright strands of newly-erected barbed wire which stretched across the entrance to the bridleway.

"Would you believe it," she said in a furious voice, "the swine's wired us off!" Scandalised, she jumped down from the chestnut and began to untwist the ends of the wire with her bare hands, watched anxiously by her pupils as they struggled to prevent their ponies from grazing the roadside grass.

I didn't like the look of this. "Francesca," I called, "wouldn't it be less trouble to keep to the roads?"

"Keep to the roads?" Along the wintry skeleton of the hedgerow, Francesca glared at me. "You can keep to the roads, Kathryn, if you like, but *I'm* using the bridleway!"

Several velvet-capped heads turned in my direction in order to observe my reaction to this fevered response, but I just shrugged in acquiescence. My life had recently been too full of conflict to enable me to enter lightly into argument.

With Francesca back in the saddle and the wire left

looped provocatively over a convenient bough, we rode onto the bridleway. It was not an auspicious start to a Saturday morning, and as the children fell into casual groups of twos and threes in order to resume their chatter, Francesca stood in her stirrups and hawked the surrounding area for any sign of her opponent. Her manner was uncompromisingly militant and I hoped there would not be a confrontation. I wanted no part in other people's hostilities.

Since I had come to Pond Cottage Riding School, I had determined not to think about Oliver, but I had not succeeded. He had been lodged in my heart, immovable as a piece of grit, and I thought of him obsessively. I had even thought to write to him, begging that there be no enmity between us, apologising for the things I had said, for the deceitful way in which I had plotted to leave him. I had even addressed an envelope, marking it 'personal' in firm, brave script, but that had been before I had visualised him opening it, slitting the top with the deersfoot paper knife he used for his own private correspondence, scanning the page with cool, negligent eyes, putting it aside as just another letter to be answered later out of duty or common politeness with something briefly adequate, dictating to the waiting John Englehart, whose typing was sure to be so much better than mine. I didn't write the letter. I tore up the envelope.

Even now, staring across the endless brown acres which stretched on either side of the bridleway, I was unable to prevent other pictures forming in my mind; pictures of dressage horses cantering to the achingly beautiful music of Beethoven; pictures of Oliver and San Domingo sweeping into extension across the diagonal in a movement so technically brilliant, yet so spontaneously joyful, that my heart was wrung to remember it; and pictures of fenced and husbanded acres of lush and verdant pasture – I had not realised until I had returned to this landscape of mud and plough laced with the dead wood of winter, how hungry one could become for green.

I forced my attention back to the present giving Davina some of the promised instruction, demonstrating simple exercises designed to relax shoulders, arms, wrists and hands. There was precious little comfort to be drawn from the past, and no profit whatsoever to be gained from speculation about what might have been. I had to accept that things were unalterably the way they were, and that Oliver was now what he had become. And yet what *had* Oliver become? I wondered if I really knew. I wondered if I really wanted to know.

I shortened the reins for my clumsily-fingered beginner infant and in the course of this I noticed that the sun had broken through the cloud for the first time in days and, glancing over a hedge as we traversed a headland beside a wide, bramble-filled ditch, I saw that the vast and rolling acres were miraculously hazed over with the ethereal green of growing seed. Riding along on the pink-nosed cob behind the chattering line of children with the sunshine drying my jersey, with the ponies' hooves rattling loose flints from the path, with a slight steam beginning to rise from swaying, rounded rumps, I told myself firmly that if this was how my life was going to be from now on, I had better find something to like about it. Surely, given time, I could cut Oliver out of my life. Francesca had managed to do it, and so could I and riding school work need not always be so grim. Already the weather had started to improve, soon the ground would dry, the mud would be a thing of the past, even the grass would grow eventually. Why, life would almost become tolerable.

Cheered by these thoughts I smiled down at my infant beginner whose face, flushed by fresh air and enjoyment, beamed up at me, as pink and as round as a little balloon. I was not at all prepared for what happened next, for what did happen next was that there was a sudden and ear-shattering explosion just behind the hedge.

For a split second nothing happened, then simultaneously, a lot of things happened at once. Like a starburst, ponies fled the spot in every direction, either riderless, or with children partially adhering to various parts of their anatomy. The fat piebald leapt into the air, swerved away into the plough, dragged the leading rein from my grasp, and began to negotiate the furrows by means of rapid bunny hops whilst my beginner infant wobbled perilously in the saddle. Davina's dun whirled round several times and vanished backwards into the ditch from whence it instantly reappeared, wild-eyed and beset by brambles, scrabbling with its front hooves to gain a purchase on the bank with Davina clinging grimly to its neck, whilst the pink-nosed cob accelerated away from the spot backwards. His determined and energetic progress was only arrested when his rump came into unexpected contact with a vehicle which, unremarked in the pandemonium, had driven up behind us on the bridleway. The horse was so astonished, and his leap into forward motion was so abruptly executed, that I fell off backwards over his tail and landed on the bonnet of a Land Rover.

I had barely managed to slide to the ground, in a somewhat shocked and defensive state, when Francesca, whose horse had taken off at the moment of explosion like a rocket-assisted jet, pursued involuntarily by her beginner mount because she could not or would not relinquish the leading rein, came galloping out of the commotion like an apocalyptic avenger, bearing down upon us with the chestnut awash with sweat, its nostrils showing vermillion and its eyes rotating crazily in their sockets. She hauled the horse to a halt inches from the vehicle and faced the driver with a wild and passionate fury.

"My God you've gone too far this time, Simon Hooper," she screeched, "shooting at innocent children and animals on the public bridleway – I'll have you jailed for this! I'll have you put away this time, you see if I don't!"

"Now wait a minute," Simon Hooper said in a contentious voice, "I didn't shoot at anybody."

Considering that he had been behind the wheel of the Land Rover, and not behind the hedge, it seemed to me that this might well be true, but I was prevented from saying so by the arrival of Davina, her jodhpurs a mess of pulled threads and blood beading along a bramble-whipped cheek. She was dragging the dun pony who was plastered with mud and had a long blackberry briar attached to the end of his tail.

"If you wouldn't mind, Kathryn," she said in a controlled voice, "I think I would prefer to walk back to the stables."

"Oh, no you don't," Francesca snapped. "Get back into the saddle."

"Now look here you two," Simon Hooper interrupted, "you're not going to blame me for this. All I'm doing is testing a new type of crow-scarer on my own land, and there's nothing unlawful in that." One of the returning pupils hooked a pony onto the wing mirror of his Land Rover. He snatched it off angrily, flinging the reins in my direction.

The fat piebald, having worn itself out over a wide arc of plough, now came trotting back to the familiar bulk of the roan cob and by a miracle, my beginner infant was still clinging to the pommel of the saddle, albeit with a dangerously fraught countenance.

"My word," I said in what I hoped was a reassuring tone, "aren't we having *fun*?" Simon Hooper, my beginner infant and Davina looked at me as if they suspected I might have sustained brain damage.

"Are you telling me you're using a crow-scarer within inches of a public bridleway, regularly used by *children*?" Francesca stared down at Simon Hooper. Two patches of colour burned high upon her cheeks and her eyes glittered with outrage.

"I'm telling you that I'm testing a crow-scarer on my own land and that I'm perfectly entitled to do so," he said, "*perfectly* entitled."

He picked up a squalling child from the vicinity of his left trouser-leg and sat it on the nearest vacant pony. He looked entirely exasperated and upset and to make matters worse the child gripped him round the neck, refusing to be left in the saddle.

"No, No!" it shrieked, "I'm not riding Misty, I'm riding Foggy!" Practically unhinged by the passage of events it kicked him energetically in the chest with its size eleven jodhpur boots and once released, tore off into the plough where Foggy was cantering in relentless but diminishing circles, as if attached to an invisible lunge.

"Oh, my *God*!" Distraught, Simon Hooper wrenched open the door of the Land Rover and threw himself into the driver's seat. He couldn't actually go anywhere because his progress in every direction was balked by equines, and Francesca, not in the least defeated by his retreat into the vehicle, now hung down the chestnut's sopping shoulder and continued to lambast him through the window.

"Just because your father happens to own land," she shouted, "it doesn't give you licence to terrorise innocent children and ponies – they could have been *maimed*, they could have been *killed*, you could have been jailed for *manslaughter*!"

"Francesca," I protested, "nobody's been maimed, nobody's been killed as far as I can see." Now that I had recovered from the shock, I felt rather sorry for Simon Hooper, especially as the children were now back in the saddle, suffering no more than the odd involuntary hiccup, and beginning to take a lively interest in the argument raging around the Land Rover.

"I *did* put the wire across the bottom of the ride," Simon Hooper turned to me, having abandoned all hope of sensible argument with Francesca, "I put it up as a preventative measure, for your own protection, you might have been warned by that."

"Yes," I agreed, "in retrospect, I suppose we should."

I rather liked the look of Simon Hooper, he had a nice face, good cheekbones, honest grey eyes, black wavy hair worn a little too long. He was not beautiful, not elegant, not like Oliver, but, Francesca could improve her lot considerably with the help of Simon Hooper, I thought. If she could bring herself to be pleasant to him, if he could begin to see her as something other than an enemy, all of Francesca's problems might be solved. As a result of this flight of fancy I saw, not only a satisfactory love affair, but horses' heads over the rows of the empty loose boxes beside the uninhabited farmhouse at Moor Park, the linking of bridleways to provide miles of uninterrupted riding, bins filled with corn, barns stuffed with hay and straw. No wonder, I thought, the ambition of every landless horsewoman is to marry a farmer.

"But you can't put wire across a public bridleway," Francesca cried, "it's illegal!" Across the bonnet of the Land Rover she scowled at me, sensing treachery.

Simon Hooper took advantage of this momentary lapse of attention to make his escape. He started up the Land Rover. As the engine roared into life, the chestnut jumped backwards in dismay, nearly unseating Francesca as its back legs sank into the plough. Somehow I managed to drag the roan cob, the dun and the fat piebald out of the way as the vehicle lurched forward, but I could only stand by and watch as an aged brown mare, ill-advisedly tied to the rear bumper whilst her rider answered an urgent call of nature behind the hedge, had the bridle snatched off her face.

"Francesca," I shouted, "the bridle!"

Francesca, grabbing at loose reins, thrusting for lost stirrups, set the chestnut leaping hysterically after the Land Rover. "Stop, you stupid fool!" she yelled, "you've got my bridle!"

She made a few spectular, but abortive lunges down

the chestnut's neck in the direction of the flying leatherwork, but Simon Hooper was not to be arrested. He accelerated away at top speed.

I used my belt as a choke halter to lead the aged brown mare. Francesca had little to say to anyone on the ride home, but indignation radiated off her like a heat haze.

FOUR

"Now that you are here," said St. Luke, and again, "now that you *are* here," he repeated, as if stringent and sustained measures had inexplicably failed to prevent our arrival and he must now accept our presence with good grace, "perhaps you should tell me what you think of my little improvisation." By means of a claw hammer, he directed our gaze up into the church roof. "You do not think," he said with some anxiety, "that it will cause offence?"

It was difficult to know what to say. Strung out from the ancient, wormy beams above the wall-mounted pulpit was a black and sinister shape. In the gloom it could have been the flayed skin of a bullock or a gigantic bat's wing, instead of what it was; an oddment of heavy gauge polythene stretched to form a canopy, gathered at five points and secured with bailing twine. It was quite monstrous, but, "I don't think it will cause *offence* exactly," I said.

"And after all, who is there to cause offence *to*?" Francesca wondered. She glanced over her shoulder into the unlit nave as if she might unexpectedly catch a glimpse of someone – not God, in all probability. In this cold, dismal place with its still, damp, unwholesome air, it would more likely be the devil she expected to see, twitching his tail out of sight behind the black box-pews. "What is it for, anyway?" she wanted to know.

St. Luke sighed, slipping the hammer absently into a jacket pocket already torn and baggy from misuse.

"The rain has found a way in at last. One always knew it would, but one hoped, all the same . . . Somehow the vestments and the sacred text must be sheltered from the deluge."

It was typical of St. Luke that he did not say protect oneself from the deluge. "The situation worsens. At evensong on Sunday I was obliged to open an umbrella."

"How absolutely terrible. Did anyone dare to laugh?" If it had happened in our youth, when Oliver, Francesca and I had regularly attended the church, I knew we would have found it irresistibly funny.

"One could wish there had been a congregation present to find it amusing." St. Luke permitted himself a little sigh which might, or might not, have been construed as regretful.

"But surely you didn't carry on? What was the point if . . ."

The service is an offering to God," Francesca reminded me, "not to the congregation."

"Of course." But how awful it would have been, how lonely, in *this* church. I could imagine it only too well, the gloomy shadows not quite banished by the stretching, guttering candle-flames, the rain drumming upon the corrugated iron sheeting which patched the leaking, slipping thatch, the snake-like hissing of the bottled gas heaters fruitlessly warming the air for a congregation that never came. St. Luke performing the office, opening his umbrella. I wondered, not for the first time, why he continued to oppose the diocese over the closure of St. Chad's, when at his other church there was order and electricity, there was a congregation to be saved, to be warmed, to arrange flowers on the altar, to polish the brass, repair the hassocks, ring the bells, to put pound coins on the collection plate. St. Aidan's was a proper church, an essential part of a community who used it, contributed towards its upkeep and were proud of it. Why then, did St. Luke cling to St. Chad's? Did he imagine that God was more likely to be found here, in this ancient, unloved place, on these uneven, stone-flagged floors, inside these stained and flaking walls with their poor, bowed, leaded-windows, under this worm-infested, leaking roof? Or was St. Luke, as some people maintained, slightly mad?

"Would you like me to give you lunch?" It was not a pressing invitation and I would have refused, but Francesca, having shifted lessons and arranged for local help to attend to the mid-day feeding in order to visit her father, was not to be despatched after a five-minute audience. "Lunch would be very nice," she said firmly.

Reluctantly St. Luke led us outside. In the churchyard, amidst the crumbling headstones, the tumbled vases spilling blackened remains of dahlias and chrysanthemums, treading the long, bleached winter grasses that had never felt the blade of a scythe, St. Luke tapped the restoration appeal barometer in an encouraging manner, as if it might be persuaded to rise a hundred pounds on its own account. The target was forty thousand pounds but the mercury, represented by a rising red line, stopped at four thousand seven hundred and sixty-two. It was a long way short, scarcely more than one-tenth of the total required, but for a church without a congregation, it seemed to me a surprisingly large amount.

"Forty thousand pounds is a colossal sum of money," Francesca said in a disparaging voice, "you'll never raise it."

"But I shall try," said St. Luke, "and I am not alone; help may well be forthcoming from the Department of the Environment and the Country Churches Trust."

"If the diocese agree to it," Francesca reminded him.

"*When* the diocese agree to it," St. Luke waded off through the grass towards the little path which gave access to the rear of the vicarage. He had less hair than I remembered and his threadbare trousers were soaked to the knee. His tweed jacket I recognised as one given by a parishioner who, fearing the worst on hearing he had cancer, had prematurely distributed his personal effects around the neighbourhood and subsequently recovered. Many times St. Luke had tried to return it but without success.

"Why doesn't somebody convince him that it's hopeless?" Francesca muttered as we followed him along the narrow, pitted path. "Even if he does manage to raise the money, to force the diocese to agree to get the grants he hopes for. Even if he puts on a new roof, treats the timbers and brings in electricity, will anyone come even then? Does anyone else really care?"

"I really don't know," I said. But I do know, I thought, that in some ways you are truly your father's daughter, plodding round your waterlogged acres, struggling against every kind of opposition to run your own business with no hope of advancement or prosperity, and every chance of eviction. Only Oliver has prospered, I thought, and now we are all three of us estranged. We are the hopeless dregs of a family, because the end of a family was what we were. St. Luke was both uncle and Guardian to Oliver and me. We had been deposited upon him when we were too young to know it, and when he was already a widower with an infant daughter of his own. He could not have welcomed it, but it seems there was little he could do. Our father, who had fancied himself as a poet but not as a parent, and had miserably failed to provide for his wife and family, walked out of our rented home one morning without so much as a word of explanation or farewell and never returned. Our mother, St. Luke's only sister, travelled extensively in search of him until every source of money failed, but he was never heard of again. When there was no money to travel, she walked locally, endlessly, becoming increasingly exhausted, odd and depressed, until one day she was discovered floating face downwards along a peaceful stretch of the river by a petrified angler. Our family history was not something I cared to dwell upon, but we had had each other, Oliver, Francesca and I, and our childhood at the vicarage, looked after by a succession of daily helps, had been happy enough.

I had been the last to visit St. Luke. It was barely six weeks since I had called at the vicarage to enquire after his welfare, but already it seemed colder and emptier than I remembered, especially the hall with its bare, exposed tiles.

"Wasn't there a carpet here?" I said. I was positive it had been there six weeks ago, thin, faded, and worn into patches, but a carpet nevertheless. Oliver, when he had been about enough to know such things, had said it was Persian and, despite its threadbare appearance, probably worth a small fortune

"What will we have for lunch?" Francesca opened the refrigerator. The kitchen looked almost the same, the familiar pine table was still there, the ladder-backed chairs. Only the dutch dresser was missing. Francesca slammed the refrigerator door shut. "There isn't *anything* we can eat – Where's Mrs. Fernley?" she demanded.

Mrs. Fernley had been the latest in the endless line of daily helps, but, neatly managing to avoid the question, St. Luke produced a bowl containing four small eggs from a cupboard. "Would boiled eggs be acceptable?" he enquired.

"Of course they would." I found a suitable pan under the sink and half-filled it with water. In the washing-up bowl I could see traces of last night's supper which had been tinned spagetti. Tonight's supper, a solitary fish-cake, was defrosting in a saucer on the draining board. Something was not quite right at the Vicarage, I felt. "Where *is* Mrs. Fernley," I asked St. Luke. "Has she left?"

"*And,*" Francesca added, having peered through the serving hatch into the dining room, "*where* is the sideboard?"

St. Luke took the claw hammer out of his pocket and put it in the drawer with the knives and forks. One felt he was playing for time, but he was saved from having to reply because one of the eggs in the bowl exploded and the kitchen was immediately filled with the most appalling smell.

"Oh, my God!" Francesca fled to open the outside door with her hand over her nose.

"Amen," said St. Luke in a heartfelt voice.

FIVE

"Francesca," I said, "something will have to be done about St. Luke."

"Really," Francesca took hold of the grey pony's tongue and pulled it out to an alarming length. She squirted a worming syringe into its throat. "Why?"

Over the pony's stiffened neck, I looked at her in exasperation. She waited whilst the pony struggled to swallow before she loosened its tongue and wiped away grey saliva on her anorak. I clipped the log and rope back onto the headcollar. "You know perfectly well what's happening," I said. "You can't pretend it isn't any of your business."

The grey pony lifted its head, pulling up the log to its farthest extent, raising its nose in a gesture of equine disgust, displaying long, curved, discoloured teeth.

"If St. Luke wants to sell the furniture, if he choses to live like a monk, if he prefers it, why *should* it be any of my business?"

Francesca moved along the row of stalls towards her next victim. The fat piebald eyed the box of syringes and assumed an antagonistic expression with its ears pressed back against its furry neck. Unable to find the courage to kick, it tried to squash us against the partition instead. Francesca thumped its ribs and it shuffled over reluctantly, wrinkling its nose in outrage. I unclipped the log and rope.

"It isn't really the fact that he's selling the furniture that worries me, after all, it's his to sell, he can do what he likes with it." I wondered if Francesca was being deliberately evasive.

"Then why do anything about it?" She grabbed the fat piebald by the jaw and managed to force its mouth open, despite some determined resistance.

I handed her a syringe. "But surely you realise what he's doing with the money?"

Francesca discharged the syringe. "No, but does it matter?"

I buckled up the noseband of the headcollar and clipped on the rope. The fat piebald shook itself furiously as if it expected to rid itself of the smell and taste of mebendazole; as if it might fly off externally in the way that water flies in droplets from a dog's coat. "Not if you don't mind the fact that he's putting it into St. Chad's restoration fund," I said.

We had moved out into the passage, having come to the last occupant of the pony stalls and were about to move on to the loose boxes. All of the stables were old and in desperate need of repair, but inside their occupants were strapped and well fed, and the straw was carefully harvested wheat, deeply laid, with thickly banked sides.

"*What* did you say?" Clearly it had not occurred to Francesca that anything other than eccentricity and a desire for austerity was the motive for the sale of the furniture. "Are you *sure* about that?" Beneath her tousled fringe, her grey-green eyes were incredulous.

"Of course I'm sure. Where else would all the money have come from? Who cares enough? Who, apart from St. Luke, sees St. Chad's as anything other than a lost cause? And anyway," I admitted, "I telephoned Mrs. Fernley."

"Mrs. *Fernley?*"

"I knew she wouldn't have left. I suspected that her services had been dispensed with for the sake of economy and I was right. St. Luke told her he no longer needed her a month ago."

We walked to the first of the loose boxes in silence, both of us pondering over St. Luke and his obsession. I opened the lower door and took the unsuspecting bay horse by the headcollar. Francesca tore the plastic cap from the end of the syringe with her teeth, spat it into the straw, and blew back her fringe in a business-like manner.

"We shall have to find a way to stop him," she decided.

"Yes," I said.

"But I'm not sure how."

"No. Neither am I."

"We shall have to think of something."

"Oliver would know what to do." It was instinctively said without any intent to cause offence, but the flight of the syringe was abruptly arrested in mid air. Francesca glared.

"Don't ever mention Oliver's name in this establishment," she snapped.

"Sorry," I said, "I wasn't thinking. You know me, always putting my foot in it."

"Don't mention his name," Francesca warned, "don't

talk about him, don't tell me anything about him, because I don't want to know."

"Of course you don't. I do realise."

"And anyway," Francesca demanded, "since when has Oliver ever considered anyone other than himself?"

As I had only just agreed never to mention him, there was no reply I could make to this.

"Oliver cares for nobody," Francesca said in a furious voice. She shot the contents of the syringe into the bay's throat with deadly intensity. Despite this, the horse gave a sudden and violent cough and ejected the paste which landed like a grey wormcast on the front of her anorak. "Grief, Redwing, you are an awkward brute," Francesca complained.

I watched in silence whilst she scraped it off and represented it to the horse, pulling his tongue out sideways over his pointed wolf teeth, smearing the paste with her fingers as far back as she could reach. Together we held his jaws shut whilst he swallowed furiously and with deep anxiety, his ears flipping backwards with the effort of every gulp.

"I don't know what's happened between you and Oliver, and I don't want to know," Francesca said in a bitter voice. "All I know is that you've always been loyal and he's never done a sodding thing to deserve your loyalty."

I thought it prudent to stay silent. I did not necessarily agree with what she said, but I was not prepared to argue about it.

"Oliver is obscene. Oliver contaminates the ground he walks on. I shall never forgive," Francesca said, "the filthy way he betrayed and disgraced us." She hurled the empty syringe into the bucket making the bay horse start.

I did not want to listen to any of this. "It's St. Luke we are concerned about at the moment," I pointed out, "not Oliver." I picked up the half-empty box of loaded syringes and the bucket containing the spent ones and followed her out of the stable. The bay horse watched our departure with obvious relief.

Francesca strode ahead to the next box and cuffed back the excitable chestnut who, despite the fact that she alone rode him, fed him, groomed him, and loved him best of all, lunged at her in a threatening manner, snaking his neck and showing his teeth. I often wondered if she minded that he did not love her back and decided she did not. After all there were many more amenable, gentler animals in the yard she could have preferred, and still she chose to love the chestnut.

"I think we shall have to help St Luke with his fund raising," I said. "If he can see that we can raise money by other means, if he can see the red line rising, maybe he won't feel it necessary to sell the furniture." I grabbed the chestnut by the headcollar and leaned on it with all my weight to prevent him rising up onto his hind legs.

Francesca inserted her thumb and forefinger behind his wolf teeth, prized open his mouth, dragged out his tongue and administered the dose.

"Fund raising? Us?" She frowned.

"Why not?" The chestnut, enraged by the efficiency and swiftness of our onslaught, drew his head into his chest causing the glands around the cheeks of his jawbone to stand out like marbles, then snaked out his neck and grabbed Francesca's anorak in his teeth. She slapped his nose smartly in well practised retaliation and he backed off into a corner, snapping sulkily at the air with his teeth. His viciousness was largely bluff, but he could have become a tyrant in less capable ownership.

"You mean flag selling – that sort of thing?"

"Not quite. I thought we might organise things in the village, you know, a Bring and Buy Sale, a Fête perhaps, a Gymkhana . . ."

"No gymkhanas," Francesca said firmly.

"Why not?" I looked at her in surprise. Of the three things I had suggested I had thought a gymkhana would appeal most of all.

"Because." She slid the bolt of the chestnut's loose box decisively. His neighbour was the roan cob with the long, white stockings. He gave us a gentle whicker of welcome and eyed the advancing syringe with composure.

"Because of *what*?" I said impatiently. I could see that fund raising was going to be impossible if every suggestion I made was to be dismissed without good reason.

"Because there have been more than enough gymkhanas in our lives already." The roan cob, anxious to oblige, opened his mouth and swallowed the dose with equanimity.

"But that's nonsense," I protested, "why, we haven't been to a gymkhana, we haven't even *watched* gymkhana games since . . . since . . ." I tailed off as I remembered, ". . . since Bickerton," I said.

"Exactly."

The roan cob watched with benign interest as we gathered up our equipment. He walked beside us to the door in a companionable manner. It is St. Luke we are trying to help, I thought indignantly, it is St. Luke we should be thinking about, and yet it is Oliver who dominates our thoughts. "Bickerton was *ten years* ago," I said.

"Was it?" Francesca pulled open the door of the next loose box. A barren Arabian mare with spectacular looks and two large splints regarded her with caution. "It doesn't seem like ten years to me."

I handed her a syringe. The Arab mare backed into a corner.

"Whatever you say, whatever anybody says, it all started at Bickerton," Francesca said, "It was her *fault*, you know, everything was all right until he met *her*."

I sighed as I took the unwilling mare by the headcollar. This was an old argument. Francesca had never ceased to blame Charity Ensdale for the way Oliver had behaved, insisting that if she had not lured him away, flattered him, given him a taste for expensive horses, for adulation, things would not have ended the way they did. Of course, this was not necessarily true; Oliver may well have become the person he became notwithstanding Charity Ensdale, or anyone else for that matter, but the accusation was not entirely without foundation. Because Charity Ensdale took Oliver away from us when she was thirty-one years old and he was seventeen, and there was not a single thing we could do about it . . .

SIX

We had never seen Charity Ensdale until the day of the Bickerton Show, but we had certainly heard of her, who hadn't? Hunters and hacks from her yard had won practically every major prize on offer, and the Ensdale prefix was well-known in breeding and showing circles. Francesca and I had often ridden past the low, half-timbered farmhouse where she lived, breathing in the warm, musky scent of the geraniums which filled the borders and the window-boxes, reining-in our ponies to gaze enviously over the hedges at the thin-coated, graceful thoroughbreds we so coveted, when all we had were our cobby ponies. Even Oliver, in those days, had a pony; a hot, chestnut mare with two white stockings called Simpson, who flew in and out of bending poles like a startled woodcock and was unbeatable at musical poles. Fellow competitors groaned aloud when Oliver rode Simpson into the collecting ring because they knew that the first prize was as good as won. One might have imagined that some of this gymnastic brilliance would have rubbed off onto Francesca and myself, but it never did. Francesca was too hot-headed for gymkhana games, and I was thwarted by the natural sloth of my pony, The

Admiral. Oliver did try to coach us once or twice but to no avail. Francesca was short on both patience and temper, and I was soon frustrated into apathy by The Admiral's lack of enthusiasm. Oliver, swinging down effortlessly to lift a flag as the game little mare stretched her neck and streaked across the paddock, was baffled by our incompetence. "I can't see *why* you find it so difficult? It's the easiest thing in the world."

It had been memorably hot for the Bickerton Show that year. Francesca and I had sought the dappled shade of an oak tree at the far end of the exercising area and our ponies, with Simpson, were tied beneath its branches by their headcollar ropes, wafting their tails at the flies, and making half-hearted attempts to nibble bark in agreeable languor. We had braved the stifling camaraderie of the licensed marquee for bottles of light ale and cream soda and now we waited, with rising impatience, for Oliver to return with the sandwiches.

"If I had realised he was going to be this long, I would have gone myself," Francesca said in an irritated voice. She had pulled off her boots and her socks and she lay on her stomach with her feet in the air. The collar of her shirt was undone, her tie hung loose, and by means of a twig she had managed to secure her thick, auburn plaits to the top of her head. Her cheeks were flushed from the heat, her brow furrowed with annoyance as she squinted across the showground, and a burst of freckles had appeared on her nose. Despite this, Francesca had an enviable attractiveness which I had never begrudged for the simple reason that she herself had never valued it. She never cared how she looked, nor did she seek to capitalise upon the fact that her smile could melt the stoniest reserve, because mostly Francesca frowned. She was frowning now.

"Oh come *on*, Oliver! Kathryn, you don't think he could have *forgotten?*"

I shrugged, partly because the heat had taken away my appetite, and partly because my eyes were glued to an approaching horse. It was a bay thoroughbred with a coat like satin, a tail like a fall of black silk, with its mane stitched into a row of perfect buttons along the elegant length of its neck, and in the saddle – Oliver!

Simultaneously, we scrambled to our feet. Oliver rode up to us, smiling, not hurrying, sitting on the bay mare in that easy way of his, as if riding was the most natural thing in the world, as if there was nothing to it.

"Oh, what a *gorgeous* thing!"

Some people, romantics maybe, are irresistibly drawn to grey horses; others, liking a bit more show, are attracted to the fiery chestnut or the dazzling palomino. Francesca always admired a coal black horse, but all my life I have adored bay horses and this one was exquisite. Her coat was the colour of a newly-shelled conker, her mane and tail were black, her ears black-tipped, and around the eyes and nostrils where the coat faded, the skin was dark brown velvet. As Oliver loosened the reins of the double bridle, she lowered her beautiful head, positioning next to my face a large, thoughtful eye, in which the pupil waved like an anemone in a deep pool. I laid my cheek against her muzzle, her breath was warm and sweet. I thought I might possibly die for love of her.

"Oliver, where are the sandwiches?" Francesca demanded. Barefoot and indignant, she squinted up at him, "And whose horse *is* this, anyway? Where did you get it?"

From the tone of her voice one might have imagined it to be a gypsy horse, plucked in the night from its tether and discovered in the morning, lame and abandoned by the roadside.

"It belongs to Mrs. Charity Ensdale. I've been asked to ride it in the Equitation Class."

"You?" Francesca was incredulous, you would have thought that Oliver was incapable, that he had never ridden, "but you can't. How can you? You haven't any clothes."

"Of course I've got *clothes*," Oliver said, "and I'm to borrow a jacket and some long boots, although they're half a size too small, I expect they'll pinch." Looking down at my besotted face, he grinned. "She *is* gorgeous isn't she? But it appears that she has no particular talent. She doesn't jump, she's too small to race, and not bold enough for hunting. Mrs. Ensdale plans to show her as a hack."

"If she were mine, I wouldn't care if she couldn't do anything at all."

Already my expectations of the equine race were realistic. I knew it was possible to have an ugly horse who could jump higher and gallop faster than the rest. You could even have a beautiful horse who could jump higher and gallop faster than the rest, if you didn't mind the fact that it hated you, but if you had a beautiful horse who could jump higher and gallop faster than the rest, and it loved you, then the chances were that it would twist a gut, or develop navicular, and break your heart. So it seemed to me that a horse as beautiful and sweet-natured as the bay mare had no need of any particular talents, that it was unreasonable and unrealistic to expect it. Running my hands over the shimmering neck, marvelling at the softness and the closeness of the coat, I said:

"We shall never own anything half as lovely. We shall never be able to afford thoroughbred horses." It was a miserable thought.

"If you think like that, you never will." Irritated by negative thinking even then, Oliver took up the reins. "If you want something badly enough," he said, "there are always ways and means."

That's where we were different, Oliver and I. He had a ruthless streak, whereas I had no ambition to speak of. Not that I didn't have my dreams, I did. In fact, my daydreams often seemed more real to me than life itself, but I had no real expectation that any of them would come true. And if Francesca wished and dreamed, mostly she kept it to herself, and so she was careful not to lay a hand upon the bay mare, and hardly looked at it.

"Who cares about thoroughbred horses anyway," she said. "Who wants to be bothered? Think of the work involved, the mucking out, the rugging up, the corn feeds."

Our ponies lived out in the Vicarage paddock all the year round, their grazing supplemented with hay only in the severest weather. We didn't possess a rug or a bandage between us. More than anything, Francesca would have liked to own a thoroughbred, but she was not going to admit it, not now, not when Oliver had forgotten the sandwiches.

Later, after the bay mare had been returned to her owner, the sandwiches delivered, and Francesca mollified, we sat on our ponies in the deafening hubbub of the collecting ring, the smell of sweat and pounded turf in our nostrils, our shirts sticking to our backs, and having been outstripped in our own heats, watched whilst Oliver, inevitably, went on to win the final of the flag race. Our yells swelled the applause as he led the lap of honour. Simpson's white stockings flashed and flew. She threw up her head and dropped her rump like a quarter horse as Oliver reined in abruptly at the collecting ring, and grinning, tossed the rosette to Francesca. The grin changed though, to a social smile, cool and polite, as someone ducked under the ropes at his side. She was slim and immaculate, in cream trousers and a silk shirt, her fair hair, paler than Oliver's, held back by a band of tortoise-shell. A hand with a golden bracelet at the wrist went out to Simpson's foaming neck.

"Well done, Oliver," Charity Ensdale said.

Beside me, Francesca stiffened, ready to be offended even before she had been introduced. And Charity Ensdales's next remark, although probably not calculated to offend, touched a raw spot nevertheless. Forced to move smartly aside as a group of ponies and riders dived forward at the call of the steward, jostling and barging in their anxiety to be favourably placed in the first heat of the next event, she lifted her dark glasses, the better to look up at Oliver and with a quizzical expression,

"Aren't you a little *old* for all this?" she said.

It was true, of course. The time was rapidly approaching when all three of us would be too old for gymkhana games. Some of our contemporaries had already moved on – to working hunter classes, to Junior Foxhunter, even to eventing, but I heard Francesca's sharp intake of breath and for once I was able to sympathise with her annoyance, because how could we move on? Where was there for us to go on our aged and cobby ponies, lacking as we did the comfortable middle-class background, the well-heeled parents to replace them with thoroughbred horses on which to make the transition to open competition? People like us didn't move on in the horse world, they faded away, they gave up, they disappeared.

Oliver threw a leg over Simpson's neck and slid to the ground. If he felt the sting of truth, he gave nothing away. I noticed that he was taller than Charity Ensdale, his natural gracefulness somehow accentuated by the boyish jodhpurs with the frayed strappings and the short boots with the worn straps at the ankle. I must have realised before then, that Oliver was different from the spotty, lanky, all too often loutish youths of our acquaintance, but I was too used to him, he was too familiar. I had taken him for granted. I only seemed to notice from that moment, the effect he had on people, the way they responded to the easy charm, the careful politeness that much later, was to turn into elegance and coldness. But he was still the Oliver we knew then, the day he stood and smiled at Mrs. Charity Ensdale. He was only seventeen and owned nothing apart from the chestnut mare with the white stockings whose reins were looped over his arm, and yet it seemed to me, watching from the collecting ring, that he had the world in his pocket.

On the wings of fury, Francesca won her heat in the next event, racing along stepping-stones formed by means of a conveniently sliced tree-trunk with unusually charmed abandon, her grey-maned roan, Sinbad, bustling along at her side. Sinbad, whose anxious, slightly protuberant eyes, and busy nature made hectic life's smallest, most commonplace activity, was not a fast pony despite all the energy he expended. Over-compact, short-of-leg and tight-gaited, he was easily overtaken by others of more fortunate conformation. Nevertheless, in the final, as first one rival dropped between the logs with a yell of despair, and another suffered a snapped rein whilst mounting and was carried away across the ring at a crabwise trot, lunging in agonised frustration at the few remaining inches of leather dangling uselessly from the bit, Sinbad managed to scuttle to the finishing line in second place. In line for the presentation, he stood in unaccustomed glory, but would have backed away at the approach of the Steward bearing the prizes had not Francesca's sharply jabbing heels warned him otherwise. With his thyroid gaze fixed suspiciously upon the ceremonial silver-plated salver, he allowed the blue rosette to be hooked onto his bridle and followed the winner round the ring at an energetic tail-twirling canter.

This unexpected success improved Francesca's mood, but not enough to allow her to accept Oliver's amused congratulations with any grace at all.

"I can't make the rest of the games," he told us, "I have to ride-in the mare for the equitation class."

"Well yes, you would have to, wouldn't you." Francesca removed her faded velvet cap and swept upwards the damp tendrils of auburn hair clinging to her brow. "We do understand. Especially as you're a bit old, now, for this sort of thing."

"And as I'll miss the bending," Oliver continued in a deliberate tone. "One of you can take Simpson, if you like."

We both stared at him. Neither of us had ever ridden Simpson in an event, not even at the few practices we had

had together. It was unthinkable that anyone but Oliver should ride her, and shocking, in a way, that she should be so casually offered. And so instead of jumping at the chance, instead of being grateful, Francesca turned on him.

"You *brute*, Oliver, how *could* you? Just because you've been offered a ride on a useless thoroughbred!"

But my eyes slid towards the chestnut mare with the white stockings, and I thought, if he isn't going to ride her any more, if he isn't going to love her, then I must. I knew Francesca would hate me for it, but, "I'll ride Simpson in the bending," I said, "only if you promise to come back for the musical poles."

I didn't feel disloyal to the Admiral. He didn't care for gymkhana games, he wasn't built for it. His body was slow and cumbersome. He was a safe, hardy, sturdy mount, not given to spirited behaviour or flights of imagination. He had three definite paces: walk, trot and canter, but no variable speeds – the Admiral had never been known to gallop. Indifferent to most things, blind to embraces, deaf to endearment or abuse, he was entirely without vice or malice, but excessively single-minded and determined in pursuit of his sole interest in life – food. As long as it was edible, his small, bright eye missed nothing, the best clump of grass, a windblown apple, the weakest part of the fence to facilitate escape when the Vicarage paddock was bare and the hayrack empty. Despite the fact that he was what he was, I loved the Admiral, and sometimes felt ashamed of my lust for beautiful, thoroughbred horses; but although I could sympathise, in part, with Oliver's defection, I was frightened for Simpson, who had never failed him, who was different from the Admiral, and I felt responsible. And so, committed to ride her in the next event, and already regretting it, I rode the Admiral back to the shade of the oak tree, leading Simpson at his side, whilst Oliver went to Mrs. Charity Ensdale, and Francesca, feeling herself betrayed by us both, rode away in umbrage.

SEVEN

"That's Oliver's pony!"

As I trotted Simpson towards the collecting ring, the least pleasant of Oliver's rivals deliberately rode his flea-bitten grey into my path, blocking it.

"Yes," I said, "I know." I wondered if he thought I had taken the wrong pony by mistake, that I was such an imbecile I imagined it was the Admiral and not Simpson, I was sitting on.

"Does he know you're riding it?"

"Well, of course he *knows*." I gave him a withering look, not liking to be thought dishonest, as well as mentally deficient.

"You mean he's lent it to you?"

"He loaned *her*, she's a mare, not an *it*." I didn't care for Sandy Headman. I didn't like his pale, freckled skin, his small, calculating eyes, and the way his ginger hair was cut to within an inch of his scalp and shaved up the back of his neck. He had never before considered me worthy of his attention, and I didn't appreciate his presumption now. Abruptly, I turned Simpson's head aside, anxious to bring the conversation to an end.

"For the *bending*?" The calculating eyes were

incredulous. It was clear he thought I was lying. The best of the games riders were proud of their ponies, and jealously possessive of their own particular partnerships, which had often taken years of practice and ring experience to cement. If I had searched my heart, I would have found that I knew this and might perhaps have understood why someone like Sandy Headman should doubt that Oliver would hand over Simpson to someone like me, who had never shown any particular promise whilst riding the Admiral, who had never stood in line with the regular winners – because Sandy Headman would never have handed over his flea-bitten grey to anyone, not under any circumstances. He would probably have murdered anyone who tried to place a foot in her stirrup.

"Look," I said, exasperated, "Oliver offered Simpson to me for the bending because he's riding another horse in the Equitation Class and it clashes."

"Another horse? Whose horse?"

"I really don't think it's any of your business." I urged Simpson on. Sandy Headman would have intercepted, kicking his pony forward, but Simpson was quicker, ducking out to the side, causing the grey to fling up her head as high as the knotted martingale would allow, rolling yellow-ringed eyes.

"You won't win."

Angrily, I stopped Simpson and turned in the saddle. "I beg your pardon?"

"I said you won't win. It would be daft of you to think you could. The mare's too bloody good for you."

"I don't expect to win, but thanks a lot for the encouragement."

"You're welcome." He grinned, enjoying my reaction, "See you in the final – if you get that far."

In the collecting ring, people I knew greeted me with astonishment, some with envy. Others stared openly or pretended not to notice, giving me covert, curious glances. Hope lit several faces as they realised that Oliver was not competing, even though Simpson was. However Simpson, with my legs at her sides, with my guiding hand on her reins, was no longer invincible, she was now merely another unknown quantity.

Francesca was still nowhere to be seen. Oliver I didn't expect. I felt rigid with nerves and strained not to show it. Walking Simpson round the cramped little ring I felt certain that everyone could see that my whole body was shaking, and my sweating palms made the reins wet. I wiped my hands on my jodhpurs and was disconcerted to catch Sandy Headman's eye. He grinned. I looked away, trying to be cool. Oliver is always cool, I told myself, if I'm to do him justice, if I'm to do Simpson justice, I must be like Oliver, I must *be* Oliver. I tried hard to feel like Oliver, but my heart was flying as I was carried forward in the rush to be selected for the first heat, and I was even more dismayed to find myself chosen, picked out to ride to the starting line in the gymkhana ring with five other competitors, mercifully none of them Sandy Headman.

Standing at the line with Simpson's slightly ewe-shaped neck in front of me, her head, held much higher than the Admiral's familiar one, sharply alert, her ears pointing like a terrier towards the line of poles, my rigid hands caused her to protest. She lifted her forelegs into the air, plunging forward in her anxiety to be away, inciting the other ponies to burst into a false start, wasting time whilst the Steward called them back to a chorus of groans from the ringside, until he could achieve a sensible line. This time I waited with the reins loosened, my hands pressed into the short-pulled, coarse mane, conscious now, of not one, but two, rapidly thudding heartbeats. Then suddenly the ponies leapt away and I was shocked by the speed of Simpson's acceleration as the white stockings flew towards the poles and dived in amongst them. We were half-way down the line before I had recovered my wits sufficiently to gain control of a sort, dragging the mare round the end pole by her mouth, swinging out wider, far wider than Oliver would have allowed, and weaving, flying, up through the poles, re-discovering my legs and my balance until, united at last, we streaked for the finishing line with hooves thundering on either side. But not fast enough to win the heat. Another pony had reached the line ahead of us.

Knowing it must have been perfectly clear to everyone watching that Simpson was a brilliant pony handicapped by an appallingly inept rider, I wanted to hide myself away immediately, I wanted to escape, and so I allowed her to plunge straight through the crowded collecting ring, not caring who I scattered in my haste to be away from the gymkhana ring, to be back safely under the oak tree with the Admiral. I only just heard the Steward as he bellowed "First two through to the semi-final!" and turned in confusion, dragging Simpson back to a walk, as I realised that it was not over, that I had another chance. And this time, I promised the chestnut mare, leaning down her neck, rubbing her wiry coat with my knuckles, you won't have to do everything, because I'll be ready to do my part. This time I won't let you down.

It was easier to be Oliver in the semi-final. Now that I

had done it once I knew how to wait, with quiet hands, with my eyes on the Steward, leaning forward so that I should not be taken by surprise as Simpson dived away into the poles, and I was able to do my part, using my legs, my weight, my whole body instead of just my hands, swinging the mare tightly round the end pole, steering through towards the finishing line at a gallop and crossing it a length ahead of our nearest rivals. Victory was very sweet and as the yells and whistles which serve as applause for gymkhana games hotly contested died away, I looked to the ringside for Francesca, hoping that she had relented and come to give her support, and saw instead, Oliver.

Oliver sat on the bay mare and it was clear that he had not joined in the rowdiness, he was too still, too intent, for that. There was no expression on his face that I could immediately recognise; not pleasure, not surprise, nor even resentment. At that particular moment, someone at my side offered congratulations and when I looked back, Oliver and the bay mare had gone.

When I re-entered the ring with Sandy Headman and two other ace games riders for the final, the panic started to return, turning my hands to stone on the reins, causing Simpson to fret as we waited at the line. Then it was Francesca who saved me, calling to attract my attention from where she stood with two bumper ice-creams, her previous annoyance forgotten. With total disregard for the importance of the moment, she grinned across at me and I was able to grin back and somehow pull myself together, loosening my grip upon the reins, even managing to fling a challenging look at Sandy Headman as we approached the start again at the request of the Steward and were off, flying, weaving, whipping round the end pole, racing for the finish, lying along our ponies' necks, and it was Simpson, flinging out her front legs, who crossed the line first! What a triumph! And what a stupendously satisfying feeling as, with total disregard for Sandy Headman's murderous expression, revelling in the tumultuous cacophony of yells and whistles, I rode out of the ring after the lap of honour and sought out Francesca with the red rosette hooked onto Simpson's browband.

Even Francesca regarded me, over what remained of her ice cream, in a somewhat calculating manner, as if I must now be reconsidered as a person, reassessed as to my actual worth.

"You know," she said thoughtfully, "if you really wanted to, if you tried, and provided you had a better pony than The Admiral, you could trounce Sandy Headman any day of the week."

"But would I want to?" I jumped down from the saddle and loosened the girth before I accepted the soggy cornet. "And what would be the point, anyway, when Oliver is good enough for the three of us?"

"Oliver," Francesca said, squinting through groups of people towards the main ring, "is at this very moment riding the Ensdale creature in the Equitation class, unless I am very much mistaken." She presented the end of her cone to Simpson. "I suppose we had better watch?"

With Simpson trotting beside us, we made for the rails. I almost failed to recognise Oliver, he looked so different. He seemed much older and startlingly stylish in the borrowed tweed coat and the long, brown boots. Even the bowler hat suited him, and the bowler hat, in my estimation, improves very few people.

The bay mare was divine, swinging into a long, extravagant trot, gliding into a slow, rhythmic canter, galloping with a long, low stride. She was so beautiful it was almost unbearable to watch. "Oh," I groaned in a hopeless voice, "if only I had the money."

"Money for what?" Francesca frowned, "Whatever do you want money for?"

I watched Oliver bring the mare smoothly back to a canter, and from canter into trot. "To buy a horse like that, of course."

"Oh".

"Well, wouldn't you? Buy a horse like that, I mean, if you had the money?"

As the horses in the ring dropped back into walk, Francesca considered it. "No-oo, I don't think I would."

"No?" I looked at her in surprise. "Not even if it was black?"

"Not even if it was black," she decided.

"Why on earth not?" I could not imagine anyone declining to buy themselves a beautiful horse if they had the money. It seemed the obvious thing to do.

"Because I would prefer to buy myself six ponies for the same price," Francesca said.

"But what on earth would you do with six ponies?"

Francesca looked enigmatic, but was saved from having to reply by a voice behind us, "Don't you think your brother suits the mare well?" We turned to see Charity Ensdale. She seemed very glamorous to us, in her expensive, understated clothes, with her face immaculately made-up, and her smooth, blonde hair. Especially since in the horse world, apart from racing and polo which are worlds apart, personal grooming tends to take second place to equine grooming, and personal egos are fed more by producing beautiful horses than by being beautiful.

"Oh, yes," I said fervently, "I think he . . . I think *they*, look perfect."

She smiled at us both, casually confident and friendly, but her eyes returned almost at once to the bay mare and to Oliver.

"I think he could do very well for himself in the show ring. He isn't a polished rider, but he has a certain style."

"People aren't usually very polished when they haven't had any professional tuition," Francesca said ungraciously.

Charity Ensdale threw her an amused look. "He's a lot better than many people I could name who have had nothing but professional tuition."

We watched in silence as the steward invited the exhibits to parade in a smaller circle around the judge. I though he was sure to pick Oliver first, bound to, but I was wrong. He selected a girl on a chestnut horse to head the line. Charity Ensdale made no comment, but visibly relaxed as Oliver was chosen to stand in second place.

"Not bad for an unpolished rider," Francesca commented. "Is that it? Have they decided?"

"Not yet, they all have to give an individual display."

"*All* of them?" Francesca's patience was already strained by the prospect of having to watch twelve horses perform individually. "What a bore."

"You don't have to *watch* them all," Charity Ensdale pointed out, "Equitation is a bit like showing horses, it's a long-winded business. If you are not actually involved it seems rather tedious. It isn't good spectator sport."

"Not like gymkhana games, you mean?" Francesca said innocently. "Even if you are a bit old for that sort of thing?"

I caught my breath, wishing Francesca would behave herself. I had never understood her suspicious nature, never shared her instinctive distrust of strangers. And if Oliver liked Charity Ensdale, then so did I, it was as simple as that.

"I think it's thrilling," I said, "and of course, we *are* involved; we are watching Oliver."

"I rather think," Charity Ensdale said thoughtfully, as the girl on the chestnut horse rode out to give her individual display, "that one day, quite a lot of people will be watching Oliver."

We watched as the chestnut trotted away, cantered a figure eight, flew into a short gallop along the rails, slowed to a walk, halted in front of the Judge, reined back, walked forward into halt and stood four-square to allow the girl to salute. It was a smooth, mannerly, expertly ridden performance, and I could not see any way in which Oliver and the bay could improve on it. But second place is quite an achievement for a brand new partnership, I told myself consolingly, if they can just hold onto it.

We all tensed as Oliver rode out and halted the mare in front of the Judge. To our surprise, he reined her back four steps immediately, and instead of walking forward the same number of steps as is normal practice, he sent her straight into a trot, trotting slowly and sitting into the saddle until he reached the straight along the rails where he sent her into extension. It looked brilliant to me, but it was not what Charity Ensdale was expecting at all.

"What the *hell* does he think he's doing?'" she said angrily, "I didn't tell him to do any of that?"

Oliver now cantered the first loop of a figure eight with a flying change to the next. Then he let the mare out into a short and spectacular burst of a gallop before timing his transitions down perfectly until he had brought the mare to halt in front of the Judge.

"You don't actually *tell* Oliver to do *anything*," Francesca said, "mostly, he decides for himself."

"So I see." Charity Ensdale watched as Oliver dropped the reins onto the polished bay neck, and took off his hat. "That's the last time he rides any horse of mine in the ring. When he comes out, I'll break his neck."

Francesca looked across at me and grinned, delighted by the way things were going. But the Judge saw only four more individual displays before making his final selection. He did not hesitate. He brought up Oliver and the bay mare to head the line.

"Well, I'll be damned." Charity Ensdale watched the presentation of awards with pursed lips, not knowing whether to feel annoyed by the cavalier way her instructions had been disregarded, or gratified by the result. As Oliver rode out to lead the lap of honour, she left us and walked over to the collecting ring.

From where we stood, with Simpson, at the rails, we watched as Oliver reined in the bay and leaned down in order to say something. To our astonishment, Charity Ensdale threw back her head and laughed.

"Look at that," Francesca said in disgust, "So much for her breaking his neck! And you expect him to come back for the musical poles?' What a hope!"

But he did come back, returning in his jodhpurs with the frayed strappings, without the jacket and the long boots, vaulting onto Simpson as the ponies began to filter into the ring for the last gymkhana event of the day.

"Did she ask you to ride for her again?" I asked him anxiously, "was she pleased?"

"She might have been." He smiled down at my upturned face, mocking me, giving nothing away, not even asking me how I had fared in the bending, and as the music roared out over the public address system, he rode into the ring, lengthening leathers which had been shortened for me, reaching down to check the tightness of Simpson's girth.

"She did ask him," Francesca said darkly, "I know she did. She asked him and he said yes, and this is the last time he will ever ride in gymkhana games."

"No," I protested. "No, that can't be true. He would have told us. He would have told *me*."

But as I watched them, as I watched Oliver and Simpson, the way they whipped round the corner markers, the way their canter slowed to the crawl along the straight, the way they accelerated into the centre the very second the music stopped, both of them totally in tune, totally intent, in devastatingly unbeatable form, somehow I knew that Francesca was right, that it was true; that this part of our lives was over.

EIGHT

Francesca was right. After Bickerton we were finished with gymkhana games and our ponies, even Simpson, became beasts of burden only. We merely used them to transport us on our increasingly frequent journeys between the Vicarage and the Ensdale yard. I don't recall that St. Luke voiced any objection to our almost perpetual absence. He was doubtless relieved to see us occupied during the long summer holidays and the light evenings when school was finished. Possibly it absolved him from responsibility in some part, because we were certainly an inconvenience to him; a further and unlooked for encumbrance, albeit dutifully accepted, for one so single-mindedly dedicated to preserving the spiritual welfare of his twin parishes. Of course, St. Chad's still had a congregation then, the village had not started to die. The primary school was still there, the bus service ran on the hour, there was a general store, a post office. Only two of the cottages beside the green had been bought by weekenders.

We might have been less of a burden for St. Luke had we taken an interest in pastoral activities, but like so many pony-orientated youngsters when allowed complete freedom, our outside interests were minimal, our lives narrow, our activities confined to the saddle. And so we shunned the Youth Club, we scorned the tennis and the bell-ringing classes. Reluctantly, we made our token appearance in church on Sundays, and two afternoons a year we grudgingly made ourselves available to give pony rides at each separate church fête. What an unsatisfactory trio we were, and if St. Luke was unsuited to his role as paternal guardian, then how much more unsuitable were we to be his charges.

From the very beginning Charity Ensdale set out to cultivate all three of us, although there was never any doubt that it was Oliver she wanted. In retrospect, it cannot have been easy for her, because Francesca and I were well aware of our position, that we were the package deal that went with Oliver, and Francesca especially, went out of her way to be difficult. For the first few weeks she refused to accompany us to the yard. She chose to stay behind at the Vicarage, avoiding us when we returned, speaking to us only when it was necessary, at pains not to appear in the least interested in how we had spent our day. Oliver made a point of discussing our activities at meal times, because then, with St. Luke present to preside over the meal left for us by the part-time housekeeper, there was no escape, and also because he knew Francesca would be listening even though she pretended not to be. He would describe the daily progress of the novice hack we were helping to prepare for a forthcoming show, or the bungling nervousness of a small child who was taking lessons in ringcraft before making her show debut on a pony that had cost her father ten thousand pounds.

St. Luke would take no part in these conversations. Mealtimes were utilised as an opportunity to make notes for his sermons, and these he scribbled onto small pieces of papers between forkfuls.

Doth not even nature itself teach you that, if a man have long hair, it is a shame unto him? See Corinth. 12.

He had never been known to refer to these scribbled notes during the composition of his sermons, perhaps the action of writing it down helped to commit it to memory, and perhaps it did not, but in either case the pieces of paper gathered in little drifts on tables and shelves all over the vicarage until, browning and curled at the edges, they were gathered up by the home help and thrown away like so many dead leaves. And so Francesca, with nothing to scribble herself and doing her best to ignore our discussion, was forced to demonstrate her indifference by clearing away the dishes in an uncharacteristically busy manner, deliberately thumping down the cheese-board or the fruit bowl in front of us, whilst St. Luke, frowning gently over his half-glasses would murmur, "Steady now, steady," and Oliver, catching my eye, grinned.

As a result of this, one day when we were in the schooling paddock marking out a figure eight by means of a bucket of sawdust for the benefit of a particularly dense child who was unable to master the art of cantering regular sized loops, Francesca appeared, riding along the post and rail fence on Sinbad. I would have rushed across the grass to greet her, but Oliver prevented me, grabbing my wrist.

"Don't make a fuss," he said. "Don't look at her. Leave her alone. Ignore her."

So we watched covertly as she reined in at the gate, declining to enter, but making Sinbad wait for almost twenty minutes, even though he fumed and fretted to be on his way, whilst she scrutinised our industry. We did not acknowledge her presence, neither did she acknowledge us, and nothing at all was said at supper, but the following morning, three of us, not two, set out for the Ensdale yard.

It was several months before Francesca allowed herself to become totally involved in the yard. At first she was openly disapproving, resentful, and moody – often she would ride away for no apparent reason and not return. She never allowed herself to relax with Charity Ensdale, treating her with a censorious mistrust that only gradually mellowed into a sort of wary respect as all three of us were drawn deeper and deeper into the fascinating new world the Ensdale Stud opened up for us.

Charity Ensdale specialised in breeding what we had always regarded as beautiful but rather useless show ponies. They were the kind of impossibly elegant, expensive-looking creatures glimpsed in the rings at shows in the early part of the day before the hoi polloi took over, garlanded with many-tiered rosettes, their immaculate blue-coated riders looking unbearably smug as they were presented with solid silver trophies, twenty times the size of the plated egg-cups that were handed to the gymkhana champions. We had no idea, as we disapproved of them, that already many of the best games ponies, even Simpson, owed their clean lines, their speed, and their courage to years of painstaking work by the studs in order to produce a new type of pony to satisfy the demanding and competitive child of the day.

The hybrid riding pony, we discovered, was first bred as a suitable mount for the game of polo, when it was found that the larger indigenous native ponies, although some were the right size, were neither fast enough nor agile enough for the game, and neither was the tall, spindly thoroughbred sensible or clever enough, or up to weight. The answer was to cross the best of the large natives with the small thoroughbred, thus gaining the grace, speed and courage of the thoroughbred, allied to the strength, sense, hardiness and size of the native.

Breeders producing the new hybrid pony, soon realised they had the perfect teenager's mount. The polo pony became the modern riding pony, and the modern riding pony was the main output of the Ensdale Stud.

Whilst Oliver concentrated upon the hacks and hunters, almost entirely bought in as youngsters, or sent to the yard to be produced and exhibited in the ring for their owners, Francesca and I concentrated on the ponies.

From the unruly herds of two and three-year olds, the best were drawn in the autumn of each year to be produced as novices the following season. Francesca soon displayed a talent for making and breaking the youngsters, and also helped school them under saddle. For someone of her temperament, she displayed an enormous amount of patience with the ponies, and later, with the young riders we trained to show them under saddle. I never saw her punish a pony unjustly, or admonish it with an unnecessarily sharp word, she had endless sympathy with the young.

As for me, I concentrated on the conditioning, the feeding, and the presentation of the ponies, and never tired of the magic.

I loved to see how the rough, hairy, fat creatures who were brought into the stables began to shed their coats and their fat. How, as a result of judicious exercise and feeding, they changed shape and developed muscle where there had been none. I marvelled at the way linseed and rugs flattened and improved the coat, how it became hard and close and glossy. How quickly, starting with a few hairs tweaked out at every grooming session, wild thick manes and tails were tamed and the ponies learned to tolerate being bathed and strapped. How they were disciplined to stand whilst their tails were being washed, whilst every superfluous hair was trimmed out of the ears, from the nose, off the heels. How they adapted to having four steel shoes attached to their feet, and how confidence and personality developed hand-in-hand as they progressed from the lunge to the long-reins, to being backed and ridden.

As their debut neared, it was time to select the appropriate saddlery for the show ring, an extra inch might be necessary to the length of the saddle to shorten the back, or a shorter seated saddle might be needed to add the illusion of length to an over-compact animal. Fine, thin, dark bridlework was chosen to enhance the heads of the quality ponies in the exhibition classes, whilst thicker, more workmanlike leather was used to complement the plainer hunter types for the performance classes. Finally, the day would arrive when, rugged and bandaged, re-shod with lightweight aluminium plates, their manes sewn into round, hard plaits, they would be led up the ramp into the horse box and driven to the showground where they would walk into the ring to be judged for the first time. All this I loved, and the fact that the pony concerned had been produced for the showring as a saleable advertisement for the stud and was, more often than not, subsequently sold, was never the cause of more than fleeting regret, because there was always another fat, hairy creature waiting back at the yard with which to recommence the whole amazing, rewarding process.

Because we were so fascinated, so keen to learn, and so hard-working, Charity Ensdale relied on us more and more, and her husband, Charlie Ensdale, a sober, middle-aged farmer with little interest in horses, was seen increasingly less about the yard, clearly preferring to devote more time to his other farms in the area. This arrangement appeared to suit everyone, but there was one fly in the ointment, and that was Sandy Headman.

Sandy Headman had worked on Charlie Ensdale's farms during the holidays for several years but as far as we knew, he had never been asked to help on the stud, nor had he been invited to ride – the possibility might never even have occurred to him, indeed who knows if he would have welcomed it, but as soon as Oliver began to appear regularly about the farms, hacking out the show horses, sometimes with Charity Ensdale, sometime not, Sandy began to be troublesome.

Whilst he and Oliver had been in open competition in gymkhana games they had got on reasonably well. Oliver, although he never made the slightest attempt to be 'one of the lads', had earned their respect, and Sandy Headman and others like him, who considered themselves to be hot stuff, deferred to him somewhat grudgingly. There was always a lot of good-tempered banter around the collecting rings and Oliver always gave as much as he received, managing to avoid generating any resentment. He was so rarely beaten that the challenge was, no longer to be presented with the red rosette, but to cross the line before Oliver Jasny. Now, however, Sandy Headman's reluctant admiration turned to jealousy, and because he knew better than to antagonise him, Oliver was not, even then, the sort of person you crossed lightly, despite the way he looked, he took to baiting Francesca and myself.

Most of the time we went out of our way to avoid him, but there were occasions when it was impossible to anticipate when he would appear, driving past us too fast and too close on the farm roads, starting up farm machinery unexpectedly as we rode or walked past with our young ponies, sneering and laughing at us as we struggled to control and calm them, dropping corrugated tins, or shaking out polythene ricksheets in order to frighten deliberately and annoy. Eventually, because the ponies were becoming roadshy and nervous, we complained to Charity Ensdale who immediately contacted Charlie and asked him to put an end to it.

A few days after this I was helping Oliver to tack up a two-year-old he was introducing to the lunge. Charity Ensdale was in the yard with the blacksmith, a thickset, rather phlegmatic young man, both of them staring down at the front hooves of a pretty chestnut mare who was to be shown as a novice hack the following day. She had quite exceptional conformation and presence, but she was slightly pin-toed. Her hoofs had already been reshaped with the paring-knife and smoothed with the rasp, and now she was to be shod. Charity Ensdale called to Oliver, "Donald seems to think that offsetting the clips won't help. What do you think?"

Oliver walked across the yard to look. Long summer days outdoors had given him a golden tan and the sun had lightened the colour of his hair. His shirt was open at the neck and the sleeves rolled above his elbows. He was wearing dark green stretch cord jodhpurs with leather strappings that ran the length of his legs like a Newmarket apprentice. Neither Francesca nor I had asked, but both of us knew where they had come from.

"I don't think you should offset them either, it doesn't fool anybody," he said, "but I don't see why you shouldn't use a flat alloy without any clips at all."

"Now why didn't I think of that?" Charity Ensdale turned to Donald. "Can you do it? Is it possible?"

"It's possible." With a somewhat resigned look at Oliver, Donald dropped the conventional set of alloys he was holding into his shoeing box.

"I'd have to go back to the shop for them though. It's not a line I carry in the van."

"That's all right, there isn't any desperate hurry. We can go and trim the yearlings first, the plating can wait until this afternoon." She smiled at Oliver, a special, exclusive smile, which nevertheless spoke volumes to all who witnessed it. "What a surprisingly clever boy you are," she said.

"I would not have thought," Oliver replied, meeting her gaze, "that there was anything surprising about it." He did not drop his eyes, and Charity Ensdale was forced to look away first. I knew by then, of course, that she was in love with him, and that already he had the upper hand. It did not worry me particularly. It did not disturb me the way it disturbed Francesca, who could not bear to see them together, and absented herself at the faintest hint of any intimacy. Not that anything was ever displayed on Oliver's part, he was never anything but carefully polite and well-mannered, but Charity Ensdale was quite another matter.

I took the pretty chestnut mare by the headcollar and Donald, made uneasy by the emotional tension in the air, bent to pick up his shoeing box and said, quite briskly for him:

"We'll be away to do the youngsters then, Mrs. Ensdale. The plating'll have to wait until after dinner."

Oliver left us, leading away the two-year-old towards the lunging track in the schooling paddock, at the far side of which Francesca could be seen, teaching a leading-rein pony to walk independently by means of side-reins and an outstretched schooling whip. The first and most important lesson in training a leading-rein pony for the ring is to teach it to carry itself forward and straight and on a good length of lead. All is lost if the pony leans inward and crowds the leader.

As Donald and Charity Ensdale were closing the yard gate behind them I heard the sound of an approaching tractor which meant that an expected load of hay was on its way from one of the other farms. It was my job to count it into the barn and make sure it was stacked aside, away from the mature hay we were feeding at the time. I put away the mare, replacing her rugs, and went round the back of the stables to open the barn doors. Sitting on a bale, I waited in the sweet-smelling, stuffy gloom of the interior to tell the farm-hand where to stack the bales and to count them in. I never dreamed the farm-hand would be Sandy Headman.

He stood in the doorway with his thumbs stuck through the belt loops of his denims.

"So, Katie," he said, "you've been trying to get me the bloody sack, have you?"

I got up from the bale wishing that I was not alone in the yard, knowing that Charity Ensdale, Donald, Francesca and even Oliver, were out of earshot.

"Don't be stupid," I said, "you must know we didn't say it was you we were complaining about. We didn't mention any names."

Sandy Headman was shirtless, his skin was burned scarlet, his hair was shorter, spikier than ever.

"But it was me, wasn't it?" he said. "It was me you meant?" He moved forward, further into the barn.

I shrugged. I tried to keep my voice casual. "If you say so," I agreed. But I began to move sideways all the same, measuring the distance I had to cover to gain the doorway.

"Don't think you're going anywhere just yet," he said, "I've been wanting to have a little talk with you, ever since the bending at Bickerton."

I rather doubted it. After all, he had seen me many times since, when he had been roaring past me on the farm roads, rattling galvanised sheets, frightening the ponies. "Oh yes," I said, "Why?"

"Because you rode the pony bloody well, Katie. I underestimated you. I don't usually underestimate people." He moved towards me. I stiffened. I should have been ready to run past him. I wanted to get away, but my feet seemed to be glued to the floor.

He came right up to me, leaning on a bale, pulling out a straw and chewing it reflectively, not taking his eyes away from mine. I noticed that his eyebrows and eyelashes looked very pale against the red of his skin.

"That bloody precious brother of yours should have been proud of you, Katie," he said. "He *was* proud of you, wasn't he? Or was the chiselling Bastard too busy looking after Number One to notice?"

I wasn't going to listen to this. I tried to make a dash for it, but he was too quick for me. He grabbed me by my arms and pinned me back against the hay. He smelled of sweat and petrol. I closed my eyes so I should not have to look at him, but I could not stop him looking at me.

"You're very like him. Funny, isn't it?" I froze as I felt a thick finger ending in a close-bitten nail run across my cheek. "Same eyes. Same nose. Same mouth." I might have tried to scream but my throat had already closed. "Same hair." I felt the faded length of ribbon I had used to fasten back my hair come undone. "You can even ride like him when you want to."

I could not take any more. I wrenched my head aside, I tried to free my arms, to bring up my knee, to kick, but Sandy Headman was a farm labourer who lifted sacks and bales and galvanised sheets. He forced me back hard against the bales, pressing his body against mine, bringing his face so close that I could feel his breath on my cheek.

"Don't," I pleaded, "don't!" I could not do anything to stop him. "Please don't," I whispered, "*please*." I thought I was going to faint, but really, I think I would have preferred to die.

He laughed at me, his rough wind-dried lips on mine,

"You're not *frightened*, are you Katie? Don't tell me you're so bloody innocent. You must have picked up *something* from your brother . . ."

"I would stop there, if I were you, Headman." Oliver's voice, hard as steel, came from the doorway.

Sandy Headman, taken by surprise, jerked backwards and half-turned, pulling me with him, but his grip had loosened sufficiently for me to pull myself free, and I ran, not to Oliver, but as if in some way I too was a guilty party, to the other side of the barn. From our separate corners, Sandy Headman and I now stood motionless, watching and waiting for what might happen next.

"Get out of here, Headman," Oliver said in a cold and furious voice, "get out and do not come into this yard again. If you do, I shall not be held responsible for what happens to you."

Sandy Headman moved forward. He was not the type to show that he was intimidated, but something about his stance told me he knew he was not a match for Oliver. Nevertheless:

"So you're the bloody boss around here now, are you Jasny?" he enquired in an insolent tone, "Well, we'll have to see what Charlie Ensdale has to say about that, won't we?"

"You can say whatever you like to Charlie Ensdale," Oliver said quietly, "It will not make the slightest difference to me."

Sandy Headman was level with Oliver by this time and for a moment, I though he might respond violently, but he knew better than to attempt it. Instead he looked Oliver in the eye briefly in order to evaluate the truth of this statement and saw that it was so.

"You're right," he acknowledged as he walked out of the barn. "I'd be wasting my bloody time."

NINE

"You can't say you weren't warned," Francesca said defensively. "I did tell you its head would start to come up again as soon as it got excited, and now you can see that I was right. The pony isn't ready for the class, and that's all there is to it."

The pony in question threw up its head as if in agreement, but Oliver was having none of it.

"It is not a question of the pony being ready or not ready, it is a matter of having entered into a firm commitment; we undertook to exhibit an improved animal today and that we shall do – you can damn well tie its head down and work it in for an hour until it is too tired to be excited. After that, I shall be the one who decides whether to exhibit or not," he glanced at the expensively understated watch upon his wrist, "I expect the owners to arrive within the next twenty minutes."

"The owners can take a running jump," Francesca said, "*I'm* responsible for the schooling of the ponies, and I don't tie heads down as a matter of principle. In any case," she added in a contentious tone, "it doesn't work."

"It will have to work. Schooling obviously hasn't worked."

"Schooling hasn't *failed*," Francesca snapped, "I just didn't have enough time."

"And now you have even less time; you have exactly one hour before the pony goes into the ring."

An aristocratic hand, thin and spotted with age, the middle finger bearing a piece of jade set in rosy, soft-looking gold, was placed upon Oliver's shoulder in a conciliatory manner.

"My dear, you must allow that the girl is right, self carriage cannot be imposed upon any equine by artificial means," a heavily accented voice interceded, "it is only achieved by progressive training, by the acquistion of natural balance, and by the systematic development of the correct muscles. Let us admit that you are perfectly aware of it."

"Of course I am aware of it," Oliver gave Count Von Der Drehler a cool glance of acknowledgement, "but I am also aware of the fact that a promise, however foolish, has been made to the owners, and that they are due to arrive any moment with their only daughter, who is expecting to ride in the class. Perhaps you would care to explain that there will now be an interval of twelve months before they see their pony in the ring due to the fact that we have to redistribute its muscle structure?" He turned to Charity Ensdale in exasperation. "I really do not understand what possessed you to accept the animal on such a short-term arrangement. You must have realised how little we could achieve in a few weeks."

Charity Ensdale was now thinner than when we had first known her and less self-assured. Dressed simply in denim jodhpurs and a checked shirt, her hair tied back into the nape of her neck she looked like a schoolgirl. She responded irritably,

"I only agreed to take it as a favour, for heaven's sake. It belongs to a friend of a client whose custom I happen to value. I didn't feel it necessary actually to inspect the pony."

"I did not realise we were in business to distribute favours."

"I have noticed how sparing you are with yours," she said tartly. Conflict had been in the air recently, but it was hard to know why. I had the feeling that things were about to change, that something was going to happen, but I was unable to put my finger on it. Francesca maintained that it was Charity Ensdale's fault, that she had given Oliver too much freedom, had spoiled him and allowed him to dominate her, and that now she resented his authority, but I felt it was more than that.

The Count, smiling slightly, raised a placatory hand. He said:

"For the present, let us agree upon a compromise. Allow the young lady to school the pony for the time which remains to her, and if you will permit, I myself will explain the situation to the client, and after that, we will all make the decision."

It was Charity Ensdale's agreement he should have looked for, but it was Oliver he smiled at, raising an eyebrow in mute enquiry, and it was Oliver who nodded in acquiescence. At any other time I might have pondered the significance of this, but today I was to have my first ride in the ring, and I had more pressing concerns. I thought no more about it.

I had agreed to participate because the yard badly

needed another rider. Charity Ensdale disliked riding in the ring, and for this reason she had previously concentrated on the riding ponies, showing them in hand, which she much preferred, using local children as riders when it was necessary to exhibit them under saddle. Now, however, Oliver had become a leading figure in the hack and hunter classes. Photographs of him riding a succession of champions appeared with almost relentless monotony in the horse press during the season, and there was a long list of horses waiting to come into the yard.

Of course, Oliver had left school by this time, he was living at the farmhouse, and virtually running the yard. Charlie Ensdale now lived on one of his other farms. There had been talk, naturally, especially at first, but Charity Ensdale had managed to ignore it, and Oliver, as usual, gave nothing away. Francesca and I endured the covert glances, the whisperings whenever we appeared, and by degrees they lessened as the close-knit coterie of exhibitors began to accept us, chiefly because by means of our successes, we earned their respect. And we were content, as long as our ponies were in the ribbons, even though our names never appeared in the lists of winners, nor did our photographs ever appear in print.

The Count's appearance on the scene was comparatively recent. He was well-known as an instructor and a respected international dressage judge. Charity Ensdale had enlisted his help when a client whose hack we were exhibiting requested that the horse be trained for his daughter, who was now in her last year of riding pony classes and wanted to progress from hack and equitation classes, to Riding Club tests. Several days a week at first, a car and driver had brought the Count to the yard so that

Oliver and the hack should receive instruction.

Count Von Der Drehler was no stranger to the showring himself. In the past he had been a famous name, a star in the days of Olympia, White City and Richmond Horse Shows. He was old now, and rarely seen in the saddle, but he was still slim and straight-backed, and with his aristocratic, aquiline features, his white hair worn rather long and tied at the back with a black ribbon, his antique dress, and his passion for long, brightly coloured silk scarves, he still had about him the style and the glamour of another age.

With the help of the Count's tuition, Oliver had been successful in several best-trained hack classes, and it had been the client's wish that he should continue to ride and be trained with the horse in order to enter some novice dressage tests. Now the Count still came to the yard on occasion, but more often the car and driver came to collect Oliver so that he could receive instruction on one of the Count's own horses. For as the Count had pointed out to Charity Ensdale when she had complained to him about Oliver's increasingly frequent absences, it was quite impossible for a rider to know what he was asking of an inexperienced horse, unless he had first performed the movement on a fully trained animal.

It seemed clear to me that dressage was yet another completely different world. Gymkhana games had been the start of it, show horses and ponies had proved to be a new and exciting development and now here, on our doorstep, was the world of dressage, a totally new experience which we had not explored and knew nothing about.

If the perfection of the showring was sometimes partly

an illusion, created by means of small deceptions, no such deceptions were possible in the art of dressage. Oliver said that it was more like an exact science, the science of total perfection of movement, made all the more difficult because the finished result, so practised and precise, must appear relaxed and fluent.

Even I, who knew nothing, realised that there were no short cuts in dressage. It was the result of endless training, of total dedication, so that obedience, discipline, muscle-development, athletic ability and skill could be gradually developed in both horse and rider.

Due to Oliver's continued absences I had gradually taken over his riding out of the horses for exercise, and had begun to help with the schooling. Now, today, I was to ride one of the novice hacks in the ring and I was very nervous about it. Luckily, Charity Ensdale's riding clothes fitted me perfectly, even down to the size and length of the boots, and so, even if I was not feeling confident about my ability, I was at least confident about my dress; the well-cut blue coat, the cream breeches with their suede strappings, the silk stock and pin, the slim, shining boots reaching exactly to the knee.

But there was Francesca's pony to be exhibited first, and we were all anxiously standing at the ringside as the owner's daughter rode it inside the ropes. We held our breath as it performed, and breathed again when we saw that Francesca's hard work had paid off sufficiently for it to be presented with a yellow rosette. Everyone professed themselves satisfied by this, and now it was my turn.

Francesca sewed up the forelock plait and the end two at the withers, always left until the last moment to avoid the possibility of weakened hairs at the thinnest point of the mane. Charity Ensdale tacked up. Oliver supervised my riding-in.

The hack I was to exhibit had been introduced to the ring already and had been placed every time in Oliver's talented hands. She was white, which colour is not supposed to be applicable to horses who are always referred to as grey, however light their coat, but she *was* white; a silky snowy white, with that particular luminous glow some horses have that no photographer can capture, but certain oil painters of the past managed to reproduce perfectly on canvas. On her legs and her face she was speckled with black, tiny fine dots as if someone had flicked her with an inky pen or a water colourist's brush; fleabitten is the term used to describe it. Her hooves and her muzzle were black, her eyes most beautifully dark. She had exceedingly straight movement, floating and true, lovely conformation, and a sweet, obliging nature, but she was a dreamy creature who seemed permanently occupied with inner thoughts, and it was difficult to capture her complete attention for any length of time, and quite hopeless to attempt it at home in familiar surroundings.

At a show, however, it was always easier to give the impression that she had the natural presence, the special air of gaiety and lightness required of a hack (whose original and exclusive purpose was to show off the prowess and elegance of its rider in the confines of a public riding area such as Rotten Row in Hyde Park), because there was plenty to arouse her interest, crowds of spectators, strange horses, flags and marquees, noisy banter from the trade stands, not to mention the occasional accidental confrontation with main ring displays; motor cycles, sheep dogs, marching bands, even hot-air balloons sometimes.

Most exhibits become accustomed to the bustle of the show ground eventually, it is only the minority who actively dislike and are upset by the atmosphere, requiring to be lunged and ridden-in for hours before they will settle, becoming fitter and more full of themselves as a direct result of it, and posing even more difficulties for the producer. With the white mare however the reverse was the problem. We had to take care that she did not lose her artificial sparkle, her unaccustomed élan, so the riding-in period was kept brief. A short period was spent trotting in gentle circles to banish any stiffness which was the result of travelling. A few transitions were executed to give her balance and make her obedient. A little extension was attempted. After that, the riding-in was completed with a canter of a figure eight with a simple change, which means that when changing at the centre from one loop to the other the horse is drawn back into trot for a few strides and asked to canter off on the correct leading leg for the opposing circle, rather than effecting the change at the canter and in mid-air. This is the so-called flying change which is not normally required of a novice animal.

There was to be no waiting about in the collecting ring either. Oliver had so timed the riding-in that I was able to walk straight into the main ring without any protracted standing about during which the white mare might fall into reverie. I found myself inside the rails and under the eye of the judges in no time at all, having had no opportunity to let my nerves get the better of me, and without even a moment in which to properly assess the quality of the competition. I knew only that there were eleven hacks in the class, and that according to Francesca, only four other exhibits constituted any threat at all to me, and then only if the white mare's thoughts were allowed to wander.

Everything went well to start with, the mare trotted with a low, level stride, bringing her hocks under, but without going into full extension. I had been instructed to save that for the individual display. I could feel the judges' eyes upon her, and I had forgotten my previous anxiety about my ability to show a horse in the ring, all of my attention and every ounce of my concentration was summoned to display the mare to advantage, to keep the pace rhythmic, to maintain impulsion without any loss of apparent lightness, to make space amongst the other exhibits to enable the judges to see her properly, to keep an eye on the steward who was giving the instructions for changes of pace so that I could be properly prepared. It was quite a shock to see him wave, then urgently beckon as I cantered past him, and to realise that I was being called in to stand in second position in the preliminary placings, before we were sent out again individually to give our displays.

Ultimately it was I who failed her. It was I who allowed my attention to be diverted in the few, valuable, supremely important minutes which followed. It was certainly my fault, but Oliver was not entirely blameless, because it was towards him that I glanced as I pushed the white mare into extension along the rails, and it was Oliver I saw, sitting in the front passenger seat of the Count Von Der Drehler's gleaming car in its privileged ringside position, but he was not looking at me. He was listening intently to something the Count was explaining to him, describing to him with meticulous gestures of his expressive, aristocratic hands, and they were both of them rapt. It was as if myself and the white mare had ceased to exist.

I knew in that moment, of course, that Oliver was done with showing, that it was dressage he wanted, and as I realised this and felt my throat tighten and the white mare's stride flag beneath me, he looked up and saw me staring and from my expression guessed that I knew he was planning to leave us, that I knew what was happening, why things were changing, and as I turned my face away, I seemed to feel my heart drop out of my body.

The white mare was third in her class which was less than she had deserved, but more than I could have expected, because the second half of my individual display might have been better ridden by an imbecile. It surprised me, when I thought about it later, that nothing was said at the time by either Francesca or Charity Ensdale. Perhaps they did not notice. Perhaps they did not realise that I was capable of a better performance, maybe they had not expected much of me at all. It was, when all was said and done, my very first attempt at showmanship. But I knew, and Oliver knew, why I came out of the ring with the yellow rosette, instead of the blue, or the red.

TEN

Oliver had to tell us eventually, Subsequent events might have been avoided had I previously warned Francesca, but the truth was that I could not talk about it. I did not want to believe that it was true. I had almost managed to persuade myself that I was mistaken, that dressage would not take Oliver away from us, that it was just a passing interest which would fade, leaving things exactly as they were. And so I said nothing to Francesca. I just waited to see what would happen.

Because we had so many show horses in the yard, exercise was now achieved by two daily sessions, the first in the early morning, the other in the cool of the evening. All of us were involved in this, riding one horse and leading another along the lanes, never the same route twice in succession, and neither Francesca nor I minded it, it was relaxing and enjoyable for the horses and for ourselves.

There is a distinction between exercise and work as made by the professional horseman which is not always fully understood by the amateur. Schooling is work, and the horse must learn to recognise it as such, allowing the trainer his fullest attention and cooperation. Work is not the occasion for any display of high spirits or wilfulness, and discipline is always totally enforced, with the stick if necessary. Exercise is quite different. During exercise, the horse is allowed to relax, to take an interest in his surroundings, to enjoy himself, and the discipline enforced is only that laid down by safety and good manners. By this, I do not mean that the horses were allowed to misbehave on these daily exercise sessions. They had already learned that bucking, kicking and boisterous behaviour were all very well in the paddock (where all of the horses and ponies, without exception, were given an hour or two of complete freedom every day), or even on the lunge where, though not actively encouraged, spirited displays went unpenalised, but were quite out of the question when there was a rider in the saddle.

Exercise and freedom are essential if the horse is to be kept psychologically sound, but work and discipline make for performance and safety, and it is vital that the horse learns the difference between the two. The show horse who pulls himself together when he enters the ring, saying to himself, *Ah, this is work*, and out of habit, makes himself fully available to his rider, will consistently behave and perform, whereas another horse who recognises no such distinction, even though he may be every bit as beautful and as able, will throw away his chances time after time by his inattention.

It was after one of these morning exercise sessions that Oliver told us. Charity Ensdale, for reasons we would later understand, had not been out that day, and Oliver and myself had taken three horses each, riding one and leading one on either side. Thus encumbered, there had not been much opportunity for conversation, and it was not until we had carried the saddlery into the tack room that Oliver said:

"There is something I have to tell you, and I think it had better be now."

I had prayed that this moment would not arrive and I put my saddle down on the table, feeling the strength leave my arms. Francesca froze. She said in an agonised voice:

"You're not going to marry her, Oliver; you *can't.*"

It had never crossed my mind that Oliver would even consider it, and I was astonished that Francesca could believe he might. She had never voiced this fear to me, but then, being Francesca, she would have kept it to herself.

"I have not the slightest intention of marrying anybody," Oliver said.

Francesca turned to look at him, relief flooded her face.

"I am going to train for dressage with Count Von Der Drehler."

Now it was out in the open. Now it had been said. I had been warned, of course, I was half-prepared, but Francesca was not. Nor did she fully comprehend the implications of what had been said.

"We know *that*," she told him, "you've been training with him for ages."

"But now," Oliver said, "I am going to leave the yard altogether. I shall live with Eugene. I shall be his protégé."

There was a silence whilst Francesca took in this information, then:

"Leave the yard altogether?" she said in an incredulous voice, "Leave the show horses?" Her grey-green eyes widened with consternation and alarm, "But Oliver, you can't do that!"

Hooking the two snaffle bridles he was carrying onto the cleaning bracket which was suspended from the ceiling, Oliver looked at her with amusement, "And why not, may I ask? By whose permission am I to be allowed to organise my own life?"

"It isn't a matter of *permission*, it's a matter of *obligation*! What about the horses, who is going to ride them? What about the clients, how are we going to keep them without you here? What about *us*?" Francesca cried.

"Francesca," I warned, "there isn't any point in making a fuss. He will *do* it, you know he will, and we shall manage. We shall *have* to manage, and somehow, I'm sure we will."

"Of course you will," Oliver said, "some of the hunters may have to go back, but Kathryn is perfectly capable of riding the hacks, and you will still have the ponies. I am confident that you will manage perfectly well."

Francesca stared at him. Her face was flushed scarlet, and this time it was not relief, it was anger that was the cause of it.

"I see. So you are confident we will manage perfectly well, are you, just like that? Well, I'm not so confident, Oliver, in fact, I'm not confident at all," she said furiously, "I'm not even sure we even *want* to manage! I think you are forgetting who brought us here, who got us into this, because it was a step up from gymkhana games. *You* were responsible for that, Oliver, and now, because you've seen something better, you think you can walk out, leaving us to manage as best we can, leaving us to pick up the pieces, well, you can't go! You SHAN'T!"

The next minute she had hurled herself across the tackroom, flailing at him with her fists, beside herself with fury.

Oliver fended her off easily, catching her wrists, forcing her arms down, holding onto her until she gave up the struggle bursting into hysterical sobs.

"I shall go," he said in a calm voice, "so you may as well get used to the idea."

"You know we can't stop him," I said, "however much we may want him to stay, we just can't. No amount of fuss or fighting will change his mind."

"Oh, I know *that*," Francesca pulled free and backed off, rubbing her reddened wrists. "Nobody can made you do anything, can they Oliver? You always get it your way, don't you? It's always on your terms. It's always been the same. Go here because Oliver has planned it, do it this way because Oliver says so. It's never because *we* want, because *we* say, has it, Oliver?"

Oliver looked at her in exasperation, but "I suppose it has sometimes been like that," he admitted.

"Sometimes, SOMETIMES?" Francesca screamed, "It's always been like that, *ALWAYS!*"

"Francesca," I said warningly, "Francesca, don't . . ." I went to comfort her, but she would have none of it, she pushed me away. "Don't touch me, Kathryn," she shouted, "I know you're on his side? You knew didn't you? You *knew* what he was up to, but you didn't think to tell me about it? Oh no! You're just as bad as he is!" She turned venomously back to Oliver. "I *loathe* you, Oliver Jasny, I just want to be sure you know that. I think you are despicable. You brought us here, you didn't care how people talked, how they pointed fingers at us. We had to live that down, we worked hard to earn our keep, to be useful, and now what?" Her voice rose to a pitch of hysteria, "Charity Ensdale will throw us out now, that's what! But you won't care, will you, Oliver? You won't care because *you'll* be all right, *you'll* be doing DRESS-AGE!" With tears streaming down her face, she grabbed Sinbad's bridle from its peg and raced outside.

I went to follow. Oliver tried to hold me back.

"Don't go after her," he ordered, "Let her get it out of her system. She will get over it."

"She won't," I said. "Not this time." I pulled away. "You don't understand Francesca, you never have. Can't you see that she's frightened? She loves the ponies, she loves the children, and they love her. At last she's found something she *really* wants to do, that she's good at, and *you* Oliver, you haven't even *noticed*!"

I reached the paddock as Francesca, white-faced and shouting incoherently, flung herself onto Sinbad's back and set him flying towards the drive and the lane, his eyes popping with astonishment, his bushy tail twirling. The Admiral was an unsuitable mount for pursuit. By the time I caught up with them the energetic, endearing little roan was energetic no longer, he was dying on the roadside, having been hit by a car whose unsuspecting driver had had no opportunity to avoid him.

When Oliver came, and come he did, we faced him together, Francesca and I, bloodsoaked and shocked, and weeping, the dead pony lying between us. If he had shown any sign of remorse, of guilt, or compassion, we might have survived it, we might have mourned together, the three of us, but he did not. He looked down at the pony, and across it to were we stood, holding onto each other, and his face was like a glacier.

"Oh, no," he said, "do not imagine you can blame me for this. I will not be held responsible."

Less than a week later he moved in with the Count.

ELEVEN

"Simon Hooper's here, he's come to return the bridle." I put my head round the tackroom door where Francesca was dunking bits and stirrups in time to see her expression change from incredulity to annoyance.

"And there's no point in going *on*," I warned, "you might try to be friendly. It is in your own interest, after all."

"Oh," Francesca said in an unpromisingly truculent tone, "*is* it?"

Simon Hooper, in green wellingtons, cords and ancient Barbour jacket, stood in the yard holding the bridle – or what was left of the bridle.

"I don't know why you bothered," Francesca said when she saw it, "it's useless now, it must be broken in sixteen places at least."

"Fourteen," he said.

"The bit's all right," I pointed out swiftly, "we can still use that."

"The bit," said Francesca, holding up the bridle in order to display the leatherwork which was stretched, snapped and crusted with mud, "isn't a lot of use without the rest of it."

"I could offer to buy you a new one," Simon Hooper said, "but I don't think I will. It wasn't really my fault. As I don't have eyes in the back of my head, I could hardly be expected to know there was something tied to the back of my Land-Rover."

"There was pony tied to the back of the Land-Rover, and had it been wearing a nylon bridle, you could have pulled its head off," Francesca snapped, "that wouldn't have been your fault either, I suppose?"

Simon Hooper appeared to consider it. He probably realised that even nylon bridles have their breaking-point, and I could tell he found the situation ridiculous, but knew better than to smile in the face of Francesca's indignation.

"I will pay half the cost of a new bridle," he offered.

This seemed over-generous to me in the light of the fact that the bridle had been attached to his vehicle by one of our pupils and without his knowledge.

"Oh, nonsense," I said, "what does a broken bridle matter?"

"What does it *matter*?" Francesca turned to me in indignation, "Of course it *matters*" she said. "You'll be saying next it doesn't matter that he set up a crow-scarer next to the bridleway, frightening my animals out of their wits and losing me half of my regular Saturday morning clients'? I'll say it matters. Don't you care that they could have been injured? Don't you realise somebody could have been *killed*?"

I was not at all disposed to enter into that argument again, and neither, it appeared, was Simon Hooper.

"All right," he conceded, "I admit that I was responsible for the crow-scarer, and to site it so close to the bridleway was an error of judgment on my part. So to save any more argument, let me pay for the whole of the bridle, including the bit, and then perhaps we can forget the whole thing."

"Oh," Francesca said, taken somewhat by surprise by this unexpected offer, "*can* we?"

"Yes," I said firmly, "we can."

"I promise there won't be any more crow-scarers," Simon Hooper said.

"I should think not," Francesca said in an ungracious tone. "What about the wire?"

"No more wire."

Francesca did not know what to make of this. She looked at Simon Hooper suspiciously. "And the farm machinery across the rides?"

No more farm machinery across the rides."

"And ploughing the headlands?"

"I do have to *plough* the headlands," he pointed out, "but I shall be sure to leave room for the bridleway, *and*," he added, before Francesca could add to her list of grievances, "I won't put any more padlocks on the gates."

Francesca stared at him, clearly wanting to be convinced, but bewildered by the unexpected nature of all these promises, so cheerfully and willingly made, and, viewed in the full knowledge of her past difficulties, so impossible to believe.

"Why are you saying this?" she demanded. "What for? Why these promises all of a sudden?"

Simon Hooper grinned, obviously delighted to tell us, "Because I'm taking over the farm from my Father; because I'm twenty-one next week and on that day, Moor Park Farm becomes my property, and because I think it would make life a whole lot pleasanter if we were on speaking terms," he said.

Now it was me who could hardly believe it. This was the most marvellous, stupendous news. To have a friend installed at Moor Park Farm would make a world of difference to us, but Francesca was not at all impressed,

"Taking over the *farm*?" she exclaimed, her incredulous expression intimating that she didn't consider Simon Hooper capable of taking over an allotment, "*You?*"

"I'm afraid so." Unruffled by her astonishment, and perhaps even because of it, he laughed. I thought him very young to be taking over such a large and intensively cultivated farm, but then I supposed he had grown up with an interest in the land, knowing that it would be his one day, and farming it would already be second nature to him. It was always easier, I thought with a tinge of resentment, for people who inherited things. My resentment though, was short-lived in the face of his pleasure, and the future prospect of untrammelled bridleways.

"I'm very pleased for you," I said. "How lovely it must be to have your entire future so securely planned."

Francesca did not think it lovely. She did not offer any congratulation, nor did she look in the slightest degree pleased. She looked somewhat out of countenance. Instead of welcoming the news, she seemed baffled by it, offended even.

"What will happen to your father then?" she wanted to know, "Won't he come to Moor Park any more?"

"Only to visit. Moor Park isn't our only farm, you know. It's quite a way from home. We've never lived there."

"And will you live there?" I thought of the gloomy old farmhouse with its shuttered windows and its broken down conservatory, but more than that, I thought of the rows of empty looseboxes in the yard, and the empty barn, and the home paddock, bristling with thistles and docks. Life isn't really fair, I decided, whichever way you look at it.

"I hope to eventually. I shall do the old place up. I'm actually quite looking forward to it."

Fair or unfair, there was no doubt that this was encouraging news for us, but Francesca looked dismayed. In her odd, illogical way, I realised that she was going to miss the old man. The battles they had fought over the wire and the farm machinery, the shouting matches they had waged over the padlocked gates, the vitriolic letters they had sent back and forth, these had been part of her life, she had enjoyed them. I looked speculatively at Simon Hooper, trying to see in him adequate compensation for the loss of a respected adversary, but all I saw was a pleasant, cheerful, rather fortunately-placed young man, who would never have to want for much, or struggle for a living, and it was hard to see how he could be made attractive to someone like Francesca, who seemed to thrive on conflict and uncertainty. All things considered however, his take-over of the farm, and his unexpected gesture towards the establishment of amicable relations were steps in the right direction, and I felt we should now celebrate the new entente with Moor Park in some way. There was no chilled champagne at Pond Cottage Riding School, no *Tio Fino* decanted into Swedish glass. The best we could offer was the cheapest brand of the supermarket instant coffee in a chipped mug. Nevertheless:

"Would you care to join us for elevenses?" I asked him, "It's almost time."

"I should love to," he said.

We went into the tack room where I set the kettle upon the electric ring. Francesca looked slightly disapproving, making it clear that she considered my offer of hospitality excessive. Rather grudgingly, she spooned the coffee into three mugs.

Simon Hooper looked round at the saddle racks, the rows of bridles, and the headcollars with their professionally short-coiled ropes. We badly needed replacement saddlery, but the hideously wet spring meant that there would be feed bills to face long after the winter was over, and so there would be none. In spite of this, every piece of leather was soaped and supple, every bit and stirrup shone.

"What a nice harness room," he said appreciatively, "and such a nice smell."

"Tack, not harness," Francesca corrected, "harness is for driving and draught horses."

"I see. I didn't realise."

"This is a tack room," Francesca said, "a tack room usually contains saddlery, and saddlery is used on riding horses. A bridle, even a broken one, is an essential item of saddlery." Having ended her lecture on a sour note, she handed Simon Hooper a mug of coffee.

"I've always rather fancied the idea of learning to ride," he said, "but somehow, I've never got round to it,"

It was encouraging remark but typically, Francesca quite failed to take advantage of it.

"We do realise," she said in a disparaging manner, "how busy you must have been; putting up wire, setting up crow-scarers, ploughing up the bridleways."

"Francesca," I said crossly, "I thought we had agreed to forget all that."

Over the rim of her coffee cup she looked at me artlessly. "Oh yes," she agreed, "so we had."

As a celebration, it was not an unqualified success and I was obliged to follow Simon Hooper out into the yard and apologise for Francesca's attitude.

"Please try not to be offended," I said, "it's such a struggle for her to keep going at all, and the loss of even two or three weekly pupils for whatever reason, upsets her terribly. She is rather difficult at the moment, but I'm sure she will get over it if you persevere." I was afraid that he would not, that he would dismiss her as ungracious and quick-tempered which, to be perfectly honest, she often was. And yet I knew the other side of Francesca, how courageous she was, how tenacious, how immeasureably patient with her equines and her young pupils and underneath, well-hidden by her quirky humour and her suspicious and somewhat irritable demeanour, how sensitive she was, and how vulnerable.

"You will come again," I begged him, "It's been such a long-standing feud and it's high time there was a truce."

Simon Hooper paused with his hand on the gate. I noticed again what a nice face he had, and what a pleasantly uncomplicated, trustworthy person he appeared to be.

"I know I can't make amends in five minutes," he said, "I don't expect to, so don't worry that I'll give up too easily, because I won't. By the way," he added rather unexpectedly, "I don't suppose you would care to come out to dinner one evening?"

I was not sure I could handle this. I looked at him cautiously. "You are not just asking me, are you? You *are* inviting both of us?"

He looked somewhat taken aback, but he was too well-mannered to deny it. "Well, yes," he said, "I suppose I am."

"What a perfectly lovely idea. Did you have any particular evening in mind?" I thought it best to pin him down, before he had an opportunity to think about it.

"Well," he admitted "almost any night would do, I don't have a wild social life. What about Thursday?"

"Thursday is fine for me," I said, "But I will just go and make sure Francesca is available." I sped across the yard and put my head round the tackroom door. "Simon Hooper wants to take us out to dinner," I said, "would Thursday evening be all right?"

Francesca was rinsing the coffee mugs. "Don't be ridiculous," she said.

"I'm not being ridiculous, this is serious. Francesca, you will *come*," I urged.

"Why on earth should I?" She up-ended the mugs on the wooden draining board. "It's probably you he wants to take out anyway, otherwise he would have mentioned it before."

"He was afraid you would refuse," I said, "*please* say you'll accept. It's in your own interest to make friends with him, after all, and it will do us both good to go out, we never go *anywhere*."

"No," Francesca agreed, "that's true enough."

I took this to be an encouraging sign. "Then you will come? Do hurry up and tell me because he's waiting for your answer."

From beneath her untidy fringe of auburn hair, Francesca grinned at me. From behind the door I grinned back, hoping to detect a softening of her attitude.

"Of course I won't go," she said.

"*Francesca*," I said in exasperation, "you can't just refuse for no reason at all, you might be charitable enough to give him half a chance? What on earth will I tell him?"

"How about go and jump in the river?" she suggested.

It was no good. I would just have to work on her later. I went back to Simon Hooper. "Francesca says to tell you she'll be delighted," I told him.

TWELVE

The door of the Vicarage stood open to all comers, but St. Luke was not within. The hall chairs were also absent, but the circular table was still there, and on it a scrap of paper. I picked it up, thinking it might be a message.

> ". . . and there shall be a tabernacle for a
> shadow in the daytime from the heat, and
> for a place of refuge, and for a covert
> from a storm and from rain." Is.5

I could not bring myself to inspect the rest of the house, to find out what further sacrifices had been offered. I walked in the sunshine down the neglected path with its broken barleysugar edging bricks, towards the paddock. Half a dozen bullocks gambolled up to the gate in friendly curiosity. Their coats gleamed even though they had never felt a brush, and pressed together, they rubbed their curled heads against my fists. One of them raised its spotlessly pink nose and licked my palm with its rough, endless tongue. You are sacrifices too, I thought, but you will never know it.

In this paddock our childhood had been played out, and in this paddock it had ended. Here, Simpson had been found dead of a twisted gut, and on this grass The Admiral had stood, arthritic and uncaring, for the humane killer. In this paddock Francesca had planned to start her riding school, but the Diocese had refused to allow it, and now they were doubtless intending to sell it for development. It was all very melancholy, and I wished I had not come.

After the appalling incident which had resulted in the death of Sinbad, Francesca never returned to the Ensdale yard. Soon afterwards she had left to undertake a year's training at a north country equitation centre, working in return for her training, as is the custom, her living expenses paid for by St. Luke. She never saw Oliver again. She never mentioned him.

"St. Luke has told me there is some money from my Mother which will be mine when I am eighteen," she told me. "There is not much, it's hardly a fortune, but it's enough to make a start, to buy some ponies, and when I come back, when I'm qualified, I shall open my own riding school here at the Vicarage. We will do it together. I want you to promise to help me, will you promise?" I had promised.

Then there was only St. Luke and myself at the Vicarage and I was alone in the Ensdale yard. It was a difficult time. We had lost, in one fell swoop, the person who schooled the ponies, and our rider for the horses. The ponies we were already showing in the ring were not a problem. Mrs Ensdale exhibited them in hand and, thanks to Francesca's skill and newly discovered patience, the local riders who exhibited them under saddle knew their job. The ponies would be carried by their own momentum to the end of the season, and already their numbers were thinning because sales had been very satisfactory. There would be no more youngsters coming on for the present, but that could not be helped.

The horses were a different matter. I was able to ride the hacks and one or two of the lightweight hunters, and I was more than willing to do what I could, but I was still relatively inexperienced and a lightweight myself. Many people maintain that physical strength is not a necessity in a horseman, but nevertheless there were times when I was no match for a stroppy, powerful middleweight hunter. I had not the strength in the seat and legs to enable me to sit into him and hold him together, I found it hard to effect discipline. I lacked Oliver's steely nerve and his muscle. There was also the indisputable fact that the clients were expecting Oliver to prepare their horses. It was Oliver they wanted, he was the chief reason they had sent their horses to the yard after all, and Oliver had gone.

To be fair to him, Oliver had been prepared to honour his show ring commitments for the rest of the season, even though he was already riding tests on the Count's horses. The car and driver would bring him to the show in time to give the exhibit a brief riding-in within the confines of the exercising area before he rode it into the ring. Immediately after the class he would hand over the horse again and be driven away. It was obviously an impossible situation for everyone.

From necessity, Charity Ensdale accepted the arrangement for a time, but unwillingly, knowing the horses were suffering by it and, naturally, so was she. She had been badly affected by Oliver's desertion. Before he left there had been angry, emotional scenes which Oliver had countered in his usual manner with icy restraint and unshakeable resolve, so that gradually, albeit painfully, common sense had begun to reassert itself.

Charity Ensdale was still a business woman at heart, and a professional. We were in the thick of a season with several major shows still to come, and some of our exhibits already qualified for the Horse of the Year Show. We had a lot at stake, and if Oliver was not to be of use to us, then there had to be someone else. The problem was that every single rider with any talent at all was already engaged to ride. We needed an experienced rider desperately, but we did not know where to look.

"If only there was *somebody* we could think of, even somebody we could *work* on," Charity Ensdale said in despair, "I can think of any number of teenage girls, but what we need is a man, somebody who is going to look right on the horses."

I badly wanted to help. Oliver was my brother, and if she considered he had treated her shamefully, she had never allowed me to suffer by it. She could have thrown me out and replaced me with, as she had said, any number of teenage girls who would have been only too eager to take my place, but she had been generous enough not to have done so, and I had appreciated it. Now I tried to think of a way to repay her. I looked across the tackroom over the nut-brown leather of a straight-seated saddle I was soaping,

"Do you really think we might have time to work on somebody?" I asked.

She chewed her lip, pausing in the whitening of a tubular lampwick girth, whist she considered it. "Well . . . provided he was experienced enough, and provided he had proven ability to start with."

I put down my sponge. "Then I know someone," I said.

I found him on one of the adjoining farms, tinkering with the insides of a tractor which was almost past service, but still used to plough the few furrows necessary to save the hedgerows from the flames of the stubble burning. I rode up to him on The Admiral, and I waited for him to acknowledge me. For a while it did not look as if he ever would, but finally he raised his head. He did not say anything. We had not met since the incident in the barn.

"Sandy," I said, "I've come to see you because we . . . because Mrs. Ensdale . . . needs your help."

He stared up at me, narrowing his eyes suspiciously. He wore his habitual denims, baseball boots, and a filthy string vest. His ginger hair had grown longer and now stood up in a crest like a cockscomb. It was hard to picture him in the show ring but the situation was desperate and he was the only person I could think of.

"We need a rider for the horses," I told him, "and I thought you might be able to take them over for us."

"*Me*? Have you gone bloody crazy all of a sudden?" he laughed derisively, "I've never ridden a bloody show horse in my life?"

"Neither had Oliver," I pointed out.

"Ah well," Sandy Headman leaned back on the tractor and looked at me in a reflective manner. He knew that Oliver had left. Of course, everyone in the neighbourhood knew, the news had spread like wildfire.

"Oliver was different wasn't he? And I'm not Oliver, am I?"

"No," I conceded, "but I think you might do the job

very well." I looked at him critically. He was the right size for the big horses anyway, about six feet, the same as Oliver, and broad in the shoulder through labouring on the farms, yet slim through the waist and hips with, as they say in horsy circles, a good leg for a boot.

"Sandy," I pleaded, "if Charlie agrees to release you so that you can come and work for us, will you give it a try?"

He shrugged his peeling shoulders as if he could not care less, but the calculating eyes behind their bleached lashes told me a different story.

"*Please?*" I begged.

"I don't know," he said, "I might."

"Good," I said in delight, "I'll go and tell her." I clapped my heels into The Admiral's sides and surprised him into a canter.

"I didn't say I *would!*" Sandy Headman shouted after me, "I only said I bloody might!"

But he would, I knew he would, and now we had a rider for the horses. I dug my heels harder into The Admiral's ribcage, bursting to get back to the yard and break the news to Charity Ensdale.

* * *

One of the bullocks made a mournful noise as I left to find St. Luke. I had thought to find him in St. Chad's and made my way by the vicarage path. The church basked in the sunshine like an old carthorse drying the damp out of its bones. One half-expected a slight steam to rise from it. On the baked stones of the porch, three solemn little girls had set out a collection of dolls and a tiny tea-set. They were totally absorbed in their play and barely noticed as I stepped over them.

The church was not quite empty. One solitary old man sat in one of the black box pews. He was totally immobile and sat completely upright, holding his cap in his lap, and staring straight ahead. He did not appear to be praying. At least, his lips did not move, but who was I to say he was not in communion with someone.

Sunshine banished all thought of the devil. Slabs of light dropped onto the ancient stones, lit up the scarred woodwork. The poor brass shone. Someone had placed a few summer flowers on the altar. Was it so difficult after all, to see why St. Luke preferred it here? Even though it was not hushed and immaculate, and splendid like St. Aidan's? Even though there was no organ and no choir, no chandeliers and no smartly dressed ladies to organise a rota and vie with each other for the best niches in which to display their flower arrangements? Even though there were bird-droppings on the flags, and bumble bees bumping against the windows?

Out in the churchyard, a smell of mown grass, petrol and the fretful whine of a machine, indicated the whereabouts of St. Luke. I stepped back over the tea-party and took the path which led to the front of the church. One of the villagers was busily weeding a grave with a bunch of sweet peas on the grass beside her. Nearby was the grave of St. Luke's wife, Francesca's mother. That Francesca resembled her in many ways, having the same grey-green eyes, the same tumble of auburn hair, I knew from the photographs in the Vicarage drawing room and I paused for a moment at the foot of the plot, pondering the neatly tended grass, the abundant beauty of the floribunda rose, which had been chosen, Francesca had told me for the appropriateness of its name, *Sweet Repose*, and was now appreciated for its generous blooms. Was this part of the reason why St. Luke was so desperate to hang on to St. Chad's, I wondered, did he want to be laid to rest here with what remained of his wife, under the pink and gold splendour of *Sweet Repose*?

I found St. Luke struggling to cut grass by means of a hover mower not designed to cope with hummocks and patches of long, bowed grasses.

"Ah," he exclaimed when he saw me, "Kathryn." He turned off the machine which subsided with a sigh of despair. The welcome was, I fancied, a trifle apprehensive.

There was nothing to be gained by prevaricaton.

"I want to talk to you about the Restoration fund." I said.

"Ah," St. Luke said again. Beyond his shoulder I could see that the appeal barometer had risen to five thousand, two hundred and sixty seven pounds. I wondered if the rise could be attributed to the dutch dresser, the hall chairs, or both.

"I want to know," I said, "if there is really any point in fund-raising."

St. Luke pulled a grubby handkerchief from the pocket of his threadbare corduroy trousers. He wiped his brow and his hands. "What a perfectly lovely day," he said.

"I want to know," I continued, "why you don't agree to let them close St. Chad's because in the end, even if you manage to collect enough money to thatch the roof, to treat the timbers, to replace the windows, to bring electricity, who is there to appreciate it? Where is your congregation?" There had been a congregation once, I knew, because I had been part of it, but now the weekenders came and went. They had no roots in the village, their brief visits left them no time for involvement with its people. much less its impoverished, decaying church.

"Shall we sit down?" St. Luke suggested. We sat on a nearby tomb. Its stone was warmed by the sun and grainy to the touch. 'Jessica Sarah Elizabeth Obedience Barnes', one of the inscriptions read, 'Departed This Life on the 14th Day of March, in the Year 1888. Aged 37 Years. *Her Goodness Liveth.*'

"I want you to tell me," I said, "if it is sensible to try to prolong the life of St. Chad's when it will surely fall into disrepair again when you are gone and be closed by the next generation." 'Jessica Sarah Elizabeth Obedience Barnes, whose Goodness Liveth,' could be a mother to someone still living in the village, I thought, she was probably a grandmother to some, she might even be a great-grandparent of one of the solemn little girls playing in the porch. They all belong to somebody. Their ancestors lie here, their parents, their husbands, their wives, in some cases, even their children.

"I wondered, you see," I carried on, "if you think people really need St. Chad's any more? If it has fulfilled its purpose to the community it was built to serve, if it is now redundant? I wondered if it was still useful?"

Did the old man in the box pew find it useful? Why was he there, sitting with his lips not moving, holding his cap in his hands? Was he there to commune with a dead wife, or to escape from a living one? 'And there shall be a tabernacle,' I thought, 'for shelter in the daytime from the heat' or perhaps, more appropriately in this day and age, for shelter in the daytime from the world.

"St. Luke," I said despairingly, "how much money do you *need*?"

"Crabtree gave me an estimate for the roof which was ten and a half, I shall need another five." St. Luke raised his eyes to the roof in a thoughtful manner. Birds were busily pulling straw out of what remained of the thatch. The protective wire had long since rusted away.

It didn't seem such a lot. "Five hundred?"

"Five thousand," said St. Luke gently.

Five thousand pounds. More than the entire remaining contents of the Vicarage were worth, I felt sure.

"I know it sounds *impossible*," he said, "but by raising a *little* at a time . . . a coffee morning perhaps . . . a jumble sale . . ."

"A sideboard," I said, "a few hall chairs . . ."

St. Luke got up rather hurriedly.

"You are not to sell any more furniture," I said, "I . . . *we* forbid it."

He directed his attention towards the hover mower.

"You must leave *something* for Francesca," I pointed out, "God has no use for a dining table, after all."

St. Luke took the starter in his hand and pulled it. A lot of cord appeared, but nothing else happened.

"I don't know if you realise how difficult it is to have a discussion with someone who won't answer back," I said, "I know you talk to God, I know you talk to your congregation, you even talk to your parishioners, but you have never talked to us."

He unscrewed the petrol cap and peered into the tank.

"I don't wish to criticise," I said, "Neither do I wish to appear ungrateful, but you never included us, you have never wanted us close. We may not have been perfect, but you have not been without fault. You have never given us a chance to care because we have never known you. You have never *allowed* us to love you."

St. Luke replaced the petrol cap. He spent a lot of time making sure that it was tight enough.

"But, I've come to say that we want to help," I said, " I've come to tell you that somehow, we don't know how, we will help to raise the other five thousand pounds."

St. Luke straightened. He swallowed rather hard a few times, but still he had to turn his face away.

"There shall *be* a tabernacle," I said.

"You always were a *dear* child, Kathryn," said St. Luke.

THIRTEEN

"You really should let me cut a little bit off, just to trim away the split ends, it would look so much better."

"How much is a little bit?" "Show me."

Between my index finger and my thumb, I measured out approximately half a centimetre.

"Well . . ." Francesca still looked doubtful. "If you *swear* not to take off any more than that."

She had never taken a pride in her hair, never bothered to look after it, but she had always hated having it cut, even as a child. Half a centimetre was something of a triumph. The trimming scissors were reserved for the horses and locked in the tack room. I fetched bacon scissors from the tiny lean-to kitchen, where the floor glistened, unhealthy as a fevered brow, and the taps dripped ceaselessly into the stone sink. In the living room, thistles forced their way through the spongy soleplate, flattening themselves against the walls, surprising us with their sly presence whenever we moved the furniture. I began to snip away at the dry, faded ends of Francesca's hair. Neglected it may have been, but once washed and brushed out, it was lovely. Curly and strong, it trailed below her shoulderblades, and would have graced a head in a renaissance painting.

"What happened this afternoon," Francesca wanted to know, "did you manage to get any sense out of St. Luke?"

I said I thought I had.

"Well?" Francesca frowned into the plastic-backed mirror with which she was monitoring every snip of the bacon scissors. "What did he say?"

"Not a lot. You know St. Luke."

"But you did tell him we were prepared to help?"

"Yes."

"Did he seem pleased?"

"I think so." I stood back, flipping the ends of hair with a comb. I did not want to talk about St. Luke. Not yet. "Have you decided what you are going to wear tonight?"

"Not yet. But jeans, of course."

"No," I said, "not jeans, you can't possibly go out to dinner wearing jeans."

"Then you will either have to lend me something suitable, or go on your own. I don't suppose," Francesca enquired in a hopeful voice, "you *would* like to go on your own?"

"Certainly not." Hours of persuasive tactics had been necessary in order to wear down her resistance to Simon Hooper's invitation, and having finally succeeded, I was not going to allow her to back out now.

"You do realise," I said, "that we have less than half an hour in which to get ready? I think we should concentrate on finding something to wear, we can talk about St. Luke later."

"And I think you're being evasive," Francesca replied, "I think we should find something to wear, and talk about St. Luke at the same time."

We climbed the perilous little staircase where damp had gathered itself into weird, bruise-like shapes upon the plaster. Somewhat cautiously, I began to hunt through the unwholesome cupboards which tapered into the eves of my cramped, claustrophobic bedroom. Everything smelled of mice. When I had first moved into Pond Cottage, I nagged Francesca about hygiene and we had set traps and caught thirty-nine mice in one week. After that, smitten by the piteous innocence of our victims, and appalled by the growing pile of furry bodies, we had given up, hoping that some sort of ecological balance would come about. So far the balance was all in favour of the mice.

"What about this?" I pulled out a pink dress with a pleated skirt and a deep collar. It had been bought for me by Count Von Der Drehler to wear when I had accompanied him to watch Oliver perform at Goodwood, but I did not tell Francesca that. She dismissed it at a glance.

"Not pink, not with red hair. Tell me about St. Luke. I suppose you did *ask* how much he needs for the roof?"

"Umm." I turned my attention back to the cupboard.

"*So?*"

"So what?"

"So how much does he need?"

"What about this then?" I produced a white dress with splashes of red on it. "There is a belt, and somewhere, there should be a matching stole."

"I can't see myself wearing it though, can you?" She frowned at me impatiently, "Come on, Kathryn, you may as well tell me how much. Is it more than we thought? Is it hundreds?"

I found a pale green skirt in slubbed cotton. In the rickety chest of drawers under the tiny window that refused to open, I knew there was a matching angora jersey. "What about green? Surely green is all right with red hair?"

"Green will be lovely. Come, Kathryn, *tell*."

"I am not going to tell you anything until we are at dinner," I said. "It is my insurance that you will be pleasant to Simon Hooper, and that you will not take umbrage and walk out, or vanish just because you feel like it." This was not quite true. I did not want to discuss it now because once she knew what a colossal, impossible sum was involved, I was afraid she would be plunged into depression and refuse to go. At dinner, I planned to avoid the subject altogether, but at the same time, I was not averse to using any ploy which would help to show Francesca in good light in front of Simon Hooper.

With the pale green skirt clutched to her chest, Francesca looked at me and narrowed her eyes. "Just for a moment, you sounded exactly like Oliver," she said.

It proved impossible not to keep my word. Simon Hooper collected us in the family BMW and drove us out to a beamy, low-slung hostelry on the banks of the river, appropriately called The Angler. The Angler was awash with cases of flies, rods, and stuffed specimens in bow-fronted glass cases. Amidst a vast display of piscine paraphernalia, we drank an aperitif, and were ushered into a restaurant whose ceiling dripped floats of every description and whose walls were covered with angling prints.

"I thought it would make a welcome change from horse-brasses and coach horns," Simon Hooper said with a grin, as we took our places at a table with fish-printed table mats and looked at the predominantely fish menu.

As an antidote to our surroundings we all ordered baked avocado and steak. It had been a relief to see the waiter was conventionally dressed. I had half-expected him to be attired for salmon-fishing in the Spey.

Francesca looked across at me expectantly as she unfolded a linen napkin with a fishhook embroidered in the corner.

"Now, she said, "tell me about St. Luke."

I had been pleased with the effect of the green cotton skirt and the jersey. With her spectacular hair, the grey-green eyes accentuated with a coating of mascara on the lashes, the cheeks smoothed with moisturiser, and the chapped lips softened with a pink lip gloss, she looked quite stunning. Simon Hooper had clearly been taken aback by the transformation, but was far too well-mannered to say so. Now, he looked at her in consternation,

"St. Luke?" he said.

There followed some protracted explanations regarding St. Luke and his appeal fund, from which point it was possible to steer the conversation towards our childhood and family circumstances and even to Oliver and his achievements. Simon had never heard of Oliver, but as dressage does not have the popular appeal of other forms of equestrian activity such as racing, or even show-jumping, this was not surprising.

But if I had hoped that this digression would divert Francesca's attention, I was disappointed. There seemed no point in holding out, because she was determined to know.

"Five thousand pounds? Five THOUSAND?" Over

her half-eaten baked avocado, Francesca gaped.

"But I thought you said the church was eligible for some kind of grant," Simon said, "wouldn't that help towards it?"

"I don't think there will be any grants," I said, "I think St. Luke is on his own at the moment."

Francesca laid down her spoon and fork. She said in a frustrated voice,

"So there's nothing we can do to help then? Nothing at all."

"Not if you are thinking of ways to raise the whole amount." I said.

"But he will have to be stopped, you know. We shall have to stop him somehow, because he'll sell everything, he'll have nothing left, and *still* he won't have a church roof."

"But we don't have to raise the whole amount," I went on, "at least, not all at once. We will be intimidated if we look at it that way. What we have to do is to break it down a bit, to try and raise the money a little at a time."

Francesca looked at me doubtfully. "How little at a time?"

"Five hundred. Even one hundred pounds would be a start."

Francesca picked up her spoon "At this particular moment, even one hundred seems an impossibility," she said.

Simon Hooper looked thoughtful. "What do you do with your manure?" he asked.

"*Manure?*" Francesca said. The waiter who had arrived to collect our empty plates, gave her a sharp look.

"Your stable manure," Simon Hooper said, "you've

heard of stable manure, I assume? It's a waste product."

Levity was wasted on Francesca. "I know what it *is*," she told him, "it just seemed such a funny question to ask."

"Especially over dinner," I said.

"Sorry. I'm a farmer, though, remember? To me it's just another waste product, like bran, or straw. You're quite fortunate," Simon pointed out with a side-ways look at the waiter, "that I called it manure."

"What about manure?" Francesca looked at him, interested.

"The thing about manure is that it's quite valuable. You can sell manure, especially horse manure. It's a marketable commodity."

"We did try selling ours in the early days," I pointed out, "We used to stack bags by the roadside, but the Council said they were illegal and unsightly, and we had to move them."

"So we shall have to think of other ways."

Our conversation lapsed for a while to enable the waiter to serve the steak and the vegetables, to offer us french bread and mustard.

"What other ways are there?" Francesca wanted to know. "Are you going to suggest I put it in the small ads? 'Pile of manure for sale, thirty feet by sixty feet?' You do realise it's almost the size of a house?"

"Perhaps you were meaning we should try to sell it to a market garden," I suggested, "or a mushroom farm?"

"I wasn't actually." Simon fended off the waiter who was trying to encourage him to taste the wine, indicating that he would prefer to pour it himself. "Places like that are only usually interested in making regular collections from large commercial premises. You probably have a lot now, but think how long it has taken to amass it. I don't see how your few horses could make a collection contract viable."

"Perhaps we could step up production," Francesca suggested brightly, "treble the feeds, give them senna pods . . ."

I gave her a hard look. Grinning, she dropped her eyes to her plate.

"The way I see it," Simon filled our glasses with *Gevrey Chambertin*, "is that we have to work on a smaller quantity. Now and then we sell off our cow manure, but by the trailer load, just dumping it outside the houses on the pavement, but not everyone wants that much. I mean, think of all those people out there with small gardens, they want manure, but not that quantity, not for half a dozen rose bushes and a couple of marrows, all they want is a barrowload."

"Now look here, Simon Hooper," Francesa said indignantly, "if you think we're prepared to peddle manure round the suburbs with a wheelbarrow – 'Good Morning Madam would you like one lump, or two?' – you are very much mistaken."

"Not like that exactly," he said, "but what I did think was that you could pack the er . . . marketable commodity," he said, as the waiter cleared the vegetable dishes, "into bags . . ."

"Paper bags?" Francesca enquired in an innocent voice, "Or punnets perhaps? Then we could sell it like strawberries on the side of the dual-carriageway with placards set at intervals to entice passing motorists. You know the sort of thing Best Quality Manure! 200 yards ahead! Pull in now!"

"Francesca," I said warningly, "*please* . . ."

"It might sound ludicrous," Simon said reasonably, "but if you bagged it just like you did before, and advertised it as hygienically packed, well-rotted stable manure, at something like a pound a bag, delivered to the door, I think you might make a fortune."

"A pound a bag?" Francesca looked up from her steak. "Would people *really* pay that?"

"Of course they would. A tiny bag of fertilizer from a garden centre costs a bomb."

"And we've got the product," I said, "tons of it, and the barn is full of empty feed bags." It seemed a wonderful idea.

"But what we don't have," Francesca pointed out, "is the transport. How on earth are we going to deliver it door to door? By bus perhaps? Or on horseback?"

"Neither," Simon said. "You can use my Land-Rover."

In the restaurant of The Angler, at the table beside the hand-coloured print of a red mullet, beneath the dangling floats, Francesca looked at Simon Hooper, and a speculative look appeared in her grey-green eyes.

Under the table, on the pretext of smoothing the pink dress with the the deep collar and pleated skirt, I crossed my fingers briefly.

FOURTEEN

Our classified advertisement in the local newspaper was a resounding success. We had far more orders than we could conveniently cope with. All of our surplus available time was spent filling the empty paper sacks that our pony nuts were delivered in with our marketable commodity until soon we had an impressive stack of plump little bags, their tops neatly tied with baler twine. Simon, who had promised to help us to deliver the first load, looked askance when he saw it.

"I didn't realise they would be *paper* bags," he said. "I was thinking of plastic or polythene, the sort of bags we have on the farm for fertilizer."

"We're not actually selling *bags*," Francesca pointed out, "we're selling manure, I don't honestly see that it matters."

"It won't matter to the customer," Simon said, "but it might matter to you if you pick up a bag and the bottom falls out. Manure has a high water content, and the bags are only paper, after all."

Francesca scowled at him. She had not enjoyed filling the bags and had rather expected to be congratulated on her industry, not criticised for using paper instead of polythene. We loaded the marketable commodity onto the trailer, and stacked as many as we could into the back of the Land-Rover. Somehow I managed to manoeuvre Francesca in between us on the front seat so that she was sitting next to Simon. By means of plunging both pairs of her jodhpurs into a bowl of soapy water on the pretext of soaking out some of the dirt, I had managed to get her to wear jeans, and had even persuaded her to wear a soft wool jersey in eau-de-nil, which suited her perfectly. But already there was an unpleasant orange stain on one of the elbows.

A further setback occcurred just as we were driving into the suburbs. I had a street map on my lap in order to navigate the marketable commodity to its recipients and asked Francesca for the list of addresses.

"I didn't have the list of addresses," she said. "I assumed you had it."

"No, you had it before we loaded the back," I reminded her, "you were looking at it in the tackroom. It will probably be in the pocket of your jeans."

It was not.

Simon looked across at us. "I hope you haven't done anything stupid, like leaving it behind," he said.

We had.

We drove back to Pond Cottage in silence. Simon's face was grim. Francesca looked at me and shrugged her shoulders. By this time the marketable commodity was beginning to smell. The windscreen was crawling with little flies. I had the feeling that this might turn our to be one of those days one would prefer to forget.

The first address turned out to be on a housing estate too new to be on my map. This made my job as a navigator rather difficult. The estate was a labyrinth of identical streets of identical houses, liberally endowed with unexpected cul-de-sacs. We drove in rather a lot of circles. Shakespeare Drive and Chaucer Close began to look quite familiar, but Byron Avenue was not all that easy to find. When we did find it, the pensioner who answered the door required us to carry the bags down an endlessly long garden path to his compost heap. When we had each panted up and down with two bags each, he then asked us to empty out the bags so that he could inspect the contents. We stood aside and waited, whilst he poked the marketable commodity with a cane.

"If he thinks we're going to pack them up again if he doesn't want it," Francesca muttered venomously, "he's got another think coming."

She was hot and rather bad-tempered by this time, and her hair was stuck with little pieces of straw. Luckily, the pensioner professed himself satisfied.

The next customer was not at home, which necessitated a drive further into the town to the next on the list. We seemed to have used rather a lot of petrol, and with difficulty, persuaded Simon to pull in at a filling station. Petrol was more expensive than we had anticipated and this placed us in the embarrassing position of not having enough money to pay the bill. We were forced to negotiate the loan of two pounds from Simon. He was not at all grateful for the petrol, and in accelerating somewhat violently out of the forecourt, managed to lose one of the bags from the back.

"I'm beginning to wonder if this was such a bright idea, after all," Francesca grumbled as, with traffic piling up all around us, we heaved the bag back onto the tailboard. But worse was to come.

The next delivery was to a house in the middle of a long terrace, and try as we might, we could not discover the whereabouts of the back entrance. Eventually Simon drew up in front of the house and I knocked on the door, An elderly, homely lady answered and was delighted to hear that we had come to deliver her manure.

"But you can bring it straight through the house and into the back yard, my dear," she said, "It'll save you ever such a long walk with those heavy bags."

In view of the pensioner and his endless garden path, we were rather relieved to agree.

In the tiny front room, a bald-headed man with thick glasses was totally engrossed in a western film on the television with the sound at full volume.

"Don't mind my husband Arthur," his wife explained as she led us past the settee and its occupant, through the kitchen, and out into the back yard, "he's nearly stone deaf."

We had almost completed our delivery when Francesca, who was following behind me with the penultimate bag, suddenly let out a shriek as the bottom gave way, depositing a goodly portion of the marketable commodity on the carpet behind the settee. 'My husband Arthur' was sufficiently disturbed to raise his head and sniff the air. Francesca sank to her knees and frantically began to stuff the manure back into the upturned bag. Horrified, I set down my sack and went to assist.

Pistol shots reverberated around the room, hooves thundered. The cries of the wounded were deafening. Then Simon came through the front door carrying the last bag and tripped over us. The bag he was carrying split open and showered its contents everywhere. 'My husband Arthur', roused at last by a wedge of our marketable commodity, rose from the settee in confusion. All was pandemonium.

By the time we had collected up the manure and transported it into the yard, vacuumed the room, and sponged down 'My husband Arthur', we were all of us totally distraught. It was only when we were outside that we realised we had not been paid.

"We can't go back," I said, "we just *can't*, we shall have to just write it off." There was a piece of paper under the windscreen wipers of the Land-Rover. Simon pulled it out. "What is it?" I asked distractedly, "what does it say?"

"It's a parking ticket," he said, "I've been fined six pounds for parking on a yellow line."

"Six pounds?" Francesca cried in an outraged voice, "Six *pounds*?" She was quite at the end of her patience. The day had been a disaster from the very beginning, we were two pounds out of pocket, the eau-de-nil jersey was ruined, and the parking ticket was the last straw.

"Of all the senseless, idiotic things to do," she raged, "you might have known you would get a fine . . ."

Simon Hooper turned on her. So far he had managed to keep his temper in the most trying of circumstances and I would not have blamed him for venting it now. In fact, I thought for a moment he was going to strike her, but instead he took hold of her shoulders, pushed her against the side of the Land-Rover, and fastened his mouth over hers.

I tip-toed silently to the passenger door and climbed

inside. Despite everything, I could not help smiling to myself. It might not have been a good day for the marketable commodity, but it had been an excellent day for romance.

There was still, however, the problem of St. Luke. And try as I might, I could not hold out much hope for our fund-raising. But there was one person who might be able to help. That person was Oliver.

I did not want to ask him. I put it off for as long as I could but when, a few days later, Francesca went out with Simon in the evening, leaving me alone in the cottage, I sat and looked at the telephone. I knew it was stupid to feel nervous, to allow myself to be intimidated by my own brother, but at that moment I was intimidated. I was nervous. I did not want to ask him. I did not want to give him the opportunity to refuse me. As I had refused him. Four years ago . . .

FIFTEEN

Sandy Headman was very useful to the stud, and became a far better showman than I would ever have given him credit for. True, he did not have Oliver's looks, or his elegance, or his easy skill in the saddle – the kind of innate ability to make the onlooker believe the rider is doing very little apart from enjoying the ride, but he was a tireless worker who thought nothing of the heavy work around the yard, and never minded the endlessly demanding hours spent schooling the horses, or the indignity of having the rough edges smoothed off his riding in order to do them justice in the ring.

I think Charity Ensdale wondered what I had brought her at first. His appearance was so off-putting, his language was appalling, and of course, she had not seen him ride, but from the start she regarded him as something of a challenge, and gradually a working relationship developed. It amused her to try to fashion a gentleman out of such unpromising material, and she appreciated his efforts – being an extremely hard worker herself (success in the showring is never achieved by sloth), she always respected that quality when she came across it in others.

There is no doubt that Sandy Headman also had great

therapeutic value. Oliver had been an expensive emotional luxury, and his successor could not have been more different. Although at first he tried to give the impression that he was completely indifferent about it all, he was actually very proud of his new position, yet he knew his place, and was careful to keep to it. He never attempted to become over-familiar, even as he grew more confident and relaxed, and there was a welcome relief from tension in the yard. Gradually, Charity regained all her former assurance, she lost the nervous irritability which had characterised the last months with Oliver, and the fits of depression which had followed his departure lessened until they finally vanished altogether. She became once again the person she had been when we had first known her, a presence to be respected and admired, and a commanding hand upon the reins. It was all rather satisfactory.

Only one thing was less than satisfactory as far as I was concerned, and that was the gradual change in the nature and character of the yard. Any new number one rider inevitably brings with him his own special qualitites, and there was a vast difference between the qualities Oliver had, and the qualities that Sandy Headman brought to the yard. Oliver had been a skilled and aesthetically perfect horsemen, the sort of rider who improves the look of a horse simply by being in the saddle. Sandy Headman was not sublime, he looked far more workmanlike, but he was a strong rider, and fearless, exceptionally able on a difficult horse, and people in the showing world were not slow to notice that we now had one of the best nagsmen around.

As a consequence of this, the type of horses sent to us

to produce and exhibit, began to change. They were still good quality animals, still the right sort for their respective classes, but they tended to be animals with behavioural problems.

Oliver noticed the change first. He had accepted Sandy Headman's presence in the yard as a necessary convenience, and once reassured that he was no threat to my peace of mind, watched his development into a proficient showman with an ironic amusement, but; "You are getting too many rough animals," he said. "Sooner or later you are going to get hurt."

I did not believe him. "Sandy deals with the villains," I told him. "I only get to ride the mild cases. He won't put me up onto anything dangerous." This was true, because Sandy was always solicitous about my welfare. We had become friends. After some initial awkwardness which was only to be expected after the incident in the barn, there was now an easy camaraderie between us. We had achieved a relationship which would have been an impossibility under normal social conditions after such a traumatic start but which is common to the most mismatched and unlikely people when they are working together, when they are genuinely pulling for the same team.

But the work was not easy. Faults of conformation in a show horse can be disguised to a certain extent, even defective movement can be improved with sufficient care and skill, and neither of these present any threat to the producer. Behavioural problems are quite different. Manners must be imprinted upon the equine subconscious; the horse can only learn by constant repetition and has no conventional moral sensibility. Therefore good behaviour is either a habit or it is not, and all habits are more deeply ingrained if they are acquired at an early age.

The trouble was that many of the horses we were sent had not been properly disciplined in their early years and, increasingly, they were hard cases, sometimes even failures sent from other showing yards. They were certainly a challenge, but they were also hard work because when a basic obedience has not been established right from the beginning, preferably even before any formal training on the lunge or long rein, any corrective training in later years to eradicate bad habits, is a lengthy, hazardous, often distressing business, with no guarantee of lasting improvement. To give him full credit, Sandy usually managed to get them round, at least for as long as they were exhibited from the yard, but there were times when I shared Oliver's unease at the way things were going. The yard was busy, it was successful. We still had a waiting list of horses. We were paid with a bonus for every win regardless of who was in the saddle or running alongside, but I was not really happy. At any one time we would have in the yard a horse who was nappy, a bolter perhaps, a habitual rearer, an otherwise amenable animal who was a savage man-eater in the stable, and a horse with a buck capable of launching a man into space. I would have gravitated back to the ponies, but Charity Ensdale had managed to find and employ a really first-class experienced girl to run that side of things, and as such people are rare in the showing world, I knew better than to interfere with such an arrangement.

Things finally resolved themselves at a show where I was exhibiting a five-year old mare of impeccable breeding in the Ladies' Hunter Class. The mare had every possible attribute for a Ladies' hunter, she had faultless conformation, a low, long stride, she was bold and yet well-mannered with a perfectly confidential mien, but she was completely and totally ring-shy. She would do anything rather than enter the ring, run backwards into the other exhibits, rear, dig in her heels in a furiously determined jib from which no jabbing spur could shift her, or move forward as if persuaded, only to swing round abruptly in an effort to dislodge her rider. On the rare occasion when she was coerced into the ring, she would nap towards the collecting ring at every opportunity, and the whole performance would be repeated when she was asked to come out of line to perform an individual display. She was an exhibitor's nightmare and her owners, sensibly deciding that she had no future in the ring, wanted only that we should collect one or two championships at major shows before they retired her to stud. The red, white and blue rosettes were not a lot to ask and they were important because they would assure a healthy demand for her foals, but the truth of the matter was that the mare almost defeated us.

During our home schooling sessions, she had performed impeccably, lulling us with her kindly demeanour into believing her slandered by people who did not really understand horses. It was only when I tried to ride her into the ring at the first show that we realised we had been duped. It was a fiasco and, anxious to protect our reputation and not wanting to draw undue attention to the mare and jeopardise her future prospects with the judges, we removed her swiftly back to the box and drove home knowing ourselves to be fools.

From then onwards we tried every ploy we could

think of. We showed her in hand, slipping her into breed classes at local shows where she would behave with the utmost decorum, after which we put on a saddle and tried to ride her into the same ring, but she would have none of it. We tried to fake the showring atmosphere at home, by collecting as many riders and equines as we could muster and setting up a ring, but she was not deceived, she entered it like a lamb. Eventually, and with great reluctance, we were forced to resort to the stick and rattle technique. This consisted of taking her to a local show and regardless of the indignation of bystanders, meting out a punishment and at the moment of disobedience. Sandy rode her forward from the collecting ring and as soon as she hesitated he hit her hard on both sides of her flanks with a thin, elongated schooling whip, and at the same time I used the rattle, a small tin box the size of a matchbox filled with pebbles. As she went into the ring, he spoke to her kindly and rode her once round and out again. We repeated this several times, the lightning application of the long whip, and the rattle of the tin being used simultaneously, and every time the mare, horrified, entered the ring. On about the seventh occasion, we dispensed with the whip and just rattled the tin. It worked like a charm. As a corrective schooling aid, the stick and rattle is a cheat, being no solution to what is usually a psychological problem, but time was short for us and as the mare was not going to be asked to enter the ring under saddle again once the precious few tricolour ribbons had been obtained; it hardly seemed to matter that we would not achieve a lasting result.

When the Ladies' Hunter Class was called into the ring at the show where I was to exhibit her, I set her nose in the wake of another horse, rattled the box in my pocket in a warning manner, and the mare entered the ring as sweetly as a dove. She performed perfectly, was called in to head the line and gave the riding judge a delightful ride. A new rider would hold her interest for long enough to negotiate one or two circuits of the ring, and she was rewarded with the red rosette. Her owners were delighted. It hardly mattered that I was defeated in the championship by Sandy who was riding a middleweight, and had to be content with the reserve, because even that had not been expected. Everyone was happy.

The crowning incident however, occurred in the late afternoon, just as we were entering the ring for the Grand Parade followed by the presentation of prizes. Most exhibitors loathe the tradition of the Grand Parade, usually staged at four-thirty in the afternoon as a main ring spectacle to revive the interest of a flagging crowd, but for the prize winers it is a necessary event. At major shows the provision of many rings allows for the judging of several classes at the same time, but the packed schedule still demands that judging begins at eight in the morning and as the horse breeding and exhibition classes are only of interest to a minority, these are held first, before the arrival of the general public, who in the main prefer events of a more spectacular, competitive nature; show-jumping and scurry driving, punctuated by displays of sheep dogs, mounted police, or marching bands.

The variety of exhibits from the Ensdale yard; the ponies, ridden and in-hand the hacks and the hunters, meant that we had a full day anyway, and did not feel too badly about being requested to stay to parade, but a situation can arise whereby an exhibit can win its class in the early hours of the morning, and have to remain on the ground until after the parade, often six o'clock in the evening, before facing a long journey home. Small wonder then, that in the past, many exhibitors have not felt it worth their while to stay, especially as the parade can be an upsetting ordeal for youngstock and children. But most canny shows add a clause to the conditions of entry to say that should an exhibit fail to appear in the parade, their prizemoney will be withheld. It is hard on the exhibitor but essential to the success of the parade, in order to avoid a dismal procession with most of the winning animals absent, and the august personage of the show president standing beside a collection of magnificent, but uncollected trophies.

Such a clause was carried in the schedule of the show we were at; the queue of prizewinners wending its laborious way towards the main ring was interminable. The showground was packed solid with a bank holiday crowd, as Sandy, riding his hunter champion, and myself, on the grey mare took our allotted places in the crocodile which made painfully slow progress between an alleyway of people wedged ten deep towards the flags which were the only indication of the whereabouts of the main ring, and the row of dignitaries awaiting us in the grandstand. Hooked onto the bridle of the grey mare was a handsome tiered rosette with a glittering centre and gold blocked lettering proclaiming *Reserve Champion* on its fluttering tricolour tail.

It was unbearably hot and rather unfortunate that I happened to be wearing more clothing than was usual. The grey mare was exhibited under side-saddle which was to her advantage because she was not overly compact, and had a long, rangy stride, but the habit I was wearing had been tailored to Charity Ensdale's specific instructions, and was cut with an old-fashioned, distinctly feminine elegance, having a narrower waist, a more tapered sleeve, and a longer, heavier apron to ensure that it hung impeccably, and did not fly about during the gallop. This, combined with the fact that I was still obliged to wear my breeches and boots underneath, and was also encumbered with a shirt and stock knotted at my throat, plus a waistcoat and a silk hat with a veil, meant I was really rather uncomfortable, stifled by the heat, and not even able to wipe the perspiration from my brow.

Sandy rode ahead, grumbling about the narrowing gap allowed us by the press of the crowd, and the dangerous proximity of small children clutching candy floss and balloons. A small army of stewards tried vainly to widen the gap, but it was hopeless, the crowd simply moved back as soon as they moved on. In his black coat, with his confident, capable seat on the gleaming middleweight, Sandy was barely recognisable as the farm hand who had dropped galvanised sheets and shaken rick covers purposely to annoy Francesca and myself. Even the spiky hair had been tamed into a conventional haircut so that he should not disgrace the bowler hat. The middleweight pranced and sidled, his neck already showing dark patches of sweat. The grey mare followed quietly enough, only her flickering ears betraying a ruffling of her habitual composure. I found it unendurable. The mingled smells from the crowd, the bruised grass, the animals, the hot dog and the frying doughnut booths sickened me, and I wanted only for it to be over and for us to be driving back to the stud in the cool of the evening with the windows of the horsebox wound down to their fullest extent, and the horses and ponies pulling contentedly at their hay nets behind us.

Oliver, I thought enviously, would already be back at his yard. With three other of the Count's disciples, he had taken part in a display of free-style dressage to music earlier in the day. Early that morning when Sandy and I had been lunging our horses before the first of our classes, he had ridden past us on his way to the area designated for riding-in and had nodded to Sandy and grinned at me. He had been wearing white cotton breeches and a black silk shirt, and he was mounted on a black horse with white bandages. It had been noticeable that people literally stopped what they were doing for a moment in order to watch him as he rode past.

"I'd give an arm and a leg to see that sodding brother of yours look as hot and bothered as I feel." Sandy had called across to me as our horses cantered past each other, arching their necks, causing a slack to appear in the elastic-ended side reins which were attached to the rollers, swishing their still-bandaged tails. One might expect that the constantly circling animal would cause the person doing the lunging to become dizzy, but somehow it never does.

Unfortunately the free-style dressage display and my Ladies' Hunter Class had taken place at the same time in different rings, but when Sandy had seen me safely inside the rails, after he had discharged his duties as groom for the class, helping to strip the saddle off the mare and to rub up her coat before I ran her up in hand for the Judge's inspection, I had managed to persuade him to go over and watch what remained of the display so that I might hear about it after the class.

He returned to the horse-box lines soon after I had dealt with the mare, untacking her, wiping her down briefly with a damp sponge, leaving her to relax in an anti-sweat rug, with access to chilled water and a hay net.

"I wish I could say he was lousy," he had said, "but the fact is that he's bloody brilliant. He was so bloody brilliant that it was a pain in the arse to have to watch him. If I didn't know him for the swine he is, I couldn't have bloody well stood it at all."

I had already dispensed with the apron, the hat and the veil. Now I threw the jacket and the waistcoat and the stock across the bench seat in the living compartment of the horse-box, and I changed into jeans. In the shade of the box, with the main tensions of the day now behind us, we had sprawled on the grass, drinking orange juice by the gallon, laughing because Sandy had hated to admit that Oliver was brilliant.

But later, in the suffocating heat as our part of the Grand Parade crossed the perimeter of the collecting ring, when I put my hand, clad in its thin leather glove, into the pocket of the jacket to feel for the reassuring shape of the tin box, it was not there. I realised that it must have fallen out when I had thrown the jacket so carelessly across the bench seat, and rolled away unnoticed, out of sight.

Despite the heat, I felt a cold chill sweep over me. We were now almost at the entrance to the main ring with the middleweight in front, and another horse immediately behind, the crowd straining for a glimpse on either side. There was no possible way to escape. I jammed the mare's head after the tail of Sandy's horse and prayed that in all the noise and excitement, the mare would have no idea where the collecting ring ended and the main ring started. But for the interference of a well-intentioned official, I might have got away with it.

The official stepped out and, exactly at the entrance, he took the mare by the bridle, effectively halting her progress.

"Just a minute, if you wouldn't mind, Miss," he said, "give those poor beggars in the middle time to get themselves sorted, otherwise we're going to have one hell of a pile-up here."

To have been apprehended just at that particular moment was more than a disaster, because naturally the official loosed the rein to enable the mare to enter the ring, she dug in her hooves and refused to move. As I stuggled to urge her forward with my single, blunted spur, and my uselessly short whip, Sandy looked back and, seeing my predicament, mouthed silently: "Use the bloody rattle!"

"I can't," I mouthed back desperately, "I haven't got it!"

The official steward, having tried and abandoned the idea of dragging the mare into the ring, and determined to keep everyone moving at any costs, then walked round the back of the mare and, oblivious to any personal danger, clapped her soundly on the rump with his clipboard. The mare, unable to move in any direction apart from the way she was resolved not to go, rose up immediately and unexpectedly on her hind legs. For a moment her hooves flailed above the crowd, who tried to fall back only to find that due to the press from behind, they could not. A horse will not purposely strike anyone when panicked but the grey mare was perilously near to doing so because she had been unbalanced by the side-saddle. In the fraction of the second available to me, I managed to twist her head round to the front, but in doing so, I unbalanced her completely. With a hideous crash she fell over backwards.

I remember little after that apart from a confused babble of shouts and screams, but I am told that the mare scrambled up again almost at once, and that, by a miracle, I had been thrown to one side into the crowd, with the stirrup and leather, released from the saddle by a mercifully oiled and efficient safety mechanism, still attached to my foot. Vaguely, I do remember being set upon my feet, but must have fallen again directly, because when I opened my eyes I was lying on a bunk in the white vinyl-padded interior of a horse box looking up into the concerned, aristocratic features of the Count Von Der Drehler.

"Do not concern yourself, my dear Kathryn, no bones have been broken," he assured me. "It is a mild concussion only, we are convinced of that. You are not in the least damaged, and neither is the mare."

"Is Oliver here?" I had not expected the Count and his entourage to be still on the showground, and would have attempted to sit up, but the Count restrained me. Over a partition, the heads of two coal black horses looked on in an interested way.

"In all probability, Oliver is at this moment exercising the sharp edge of his tongue on your gentleman friend with the unfortunate red hair. I expect there will have been a little altercation, but you must relax now, and try not to think about it."

Try not to think about it! The last thing in the world I wanted was another confrontation between Oliver and Sandy, and I groaned aloud at the prospect. Staring helplessly up at the Count, who had a bright pink scarf wrapped around his lean neck, and a matching rosebud in the lapel of his waisted linen jacket, I said,

"He *can't* be allowed to blame Sandy for this! It wasn't his fault. If anyone was to blame, it was me!"

Before the Count could fashion a consoling reply to this, Oliver walked into the horse box. Determinedly, I struggled up into a sitting position. "Oliver, where have you been?" I demanded.

The Count excused himself somewhat hastily and withdrew. Oliver smiled. Displaying all of his easy charm, he sat down on the end of the bunk and made solicitous enquiries about my welfare.

"Don't try to avoid the question," I warned him, "I want to know exactly where you have been."

Oliver stretched out a hand and collected one of mine, pulling it towards him, staring down at it thoughtfully. Impatient for his reply, I was forced to stare crossly at the top of his head. His golden hair was lighter at the ends and dark at the roots. If I had not known him, I would have thought it was bleached, but of course, I knew that it was not.

"I have been to tell Headman that you will not be going back to the Ensdale yard," Oliver said.

I had expected this much. Angrily, I snatched my hand away.

"And I suppose you blamed him for what happened today," I said accusingly, "even though what happened was entirely due to my own negligence!"

"I did not blame anyone," Oliver said in a calm voice, "I told him his horses were dangerous, which I believe to be the truth, but I can assure you that there was no unpleasantness. I explained the situation and I am sure that he understood."

"Oh, I *bet* he did!" Incensed, I swung my legs off the bunk and made to grab for my boots. A wave of giddiness threatened to overcome me. I tried to ignore it.

"No! Listen to me!" In one swift movement, Oliver had thrown my boots to the other side of the horse box and pinned me back to the bunk by my shoulders. The coal black horses pulled back on their ropes and rolled their eyes, looking anxious. "I have something to tell you Kathryn," Oliver said and you *will* listen to me, you *will* hear me, because I shall make you."

"Now look here, Oliver," I said heatedly, "I am not going to leave my job just because you say so, because it isn't up to you to decide. When I want to leave, *if* I want to leave, I shall make the decision myself, *and* I shall give them fair warning. I am certainly not going to walk out at a minute's notice because of something that would never have happened but for my own carelessness!"

I half rose up, but was forced to lie back again almost immediately. I felt hot and weak, and totally infuriated by Oliver's presumptuous interference.

"I *shall* go back," I told him, "whatever you say."

"But you will hear me first," he insisted "Listen to me, Kathryn, Eugene . . . Count Von Der Drehler, has a vacancy in his yard. He needs someone for the young horses. The position would suit you perfectly and I know you would enjoy it. The whole place is quite beautiful. In the manège there are flowers and long mirrors, and in the yard there are doves and tumbling pigeons, and in the centre there is a fountain."

I stared up at him. I tried to imagine it.

"Kathryn, you do not need to work with Headman and his rough horses any longer, you can come with us, you can come now, today, and we will be together again. It will be better."

I looked into my brother's beautiful face, and I thought of the nappy horses, the bolters, the rearers, the ones who were savage in the stable, and the ones whose buck could launch a man into space. There was really no decision to be made. It had been taken out of my hands.

"Well, Kathryn," Oliver looked at me. "Will you come?"

I smiled up at him weakly. "You know I'll come," I said.

But I could not leave without saying goodbye to Charity Ensdale and to Sandy. Charity Ensdale made it easy for me. Typically, she brushed away my apologies, dismissing any thought I might have that I was letting her down. She had been very grateful for my hard work and my loyalty, she said, especially at the difficult time when she had lost Oliver, and she would have none of my apologies. Instead, she wished me happiness in my job with the Count and affirmed that I could not be leaving to go to a better employer. She said, and I believed her, that there were no hard feelings over my departure, that there would always be affection between us.

Sandy was not so easy. I found him in the back of the horse box, unplaiting the middleweight. He looked at me briefly with an expression I did not recognise, then turned back to the mane, snipping at the thread which secured the round, hard plaits, with a pair of sharp scissors.

"I expect you know why I'm here, I said, "I couldn't leave without seeing you, without thanking you. I have enjoyed working with you. I just wanted you to know that."

He said nothing, unwinding the plait, opening it out, combing it with his blunt fingers, picking out of it little pieces of strong brown thread.

"I just wanted to say goodbye," I said awkwardly, "and to let you know that I'm sorry to be leaving."

He moved onto the next plait. "Why leave then, Katie?" he said. "Why go then?"

"I suppose I'm going because of Oliver," I admitted, "because he wants me to. And the Count needs someone to work in the yard." I sighed, wanting to be truthful. "And I may as well admit that I'm ready for a change."

"I could change things for you," he said, "if there's something you want changing, I could change it. You only have to say the word."

He carried on snipping at the thread. His hands were large for such a job, his fingers were too thick to hold the tiny scissors properly, but as I watched him, he cut only the thread, he did not cut through a single hair.

"If it's the horses you want to change . . ."

"It isn't that," I said, "and if Oliver gave you the impression today . . . if he tried to lay *any* of the blame on you for what happened, then I apologise. I know it was my own fault entirely."

"But he's right about the dodgy horses." Sandy looked round at me and I saw with surprise how strained he looked, almost agonised. "I did have to agree with him about the horses."

"Well," I said, "well, maybe . . ."

"So I won't give you any more dodgy horses, Kate," he said, "We'll find different ones for you – ladies' horses, mannered ones."

"But Sandy," I said, "I won't be riding any more show horses, I'm leaving. I won't be here!"

"But I want you to be here," he said, "I don't want you to leave, you don't have to." To my embarrassment he looked at me almost pleadingly. "Don't go with him, Katie. Stay with us. You can trust me, and I'll do whatever you want, you only have to say the word and I'll fix it. I'd look after you. I wouldn't see you hurt, not for anything in the world."

"Of course you wouldn't." I could hardly believe that this was Sandy Headman speaking, it was so untypical.

"Bloody hell, Katie!" He turned away, back to the middleweight's frizzy mane, mortified, and full of gloom. "Look," he said, "I don't like saying this, it's bloody painful, but what I'm telling you is that he doesn't care about you, he can't, otherwise he wouldn't have left you behind before, he's going to use you, just like he's used everybody else. Oliver doesn't care a toss for anybody, but *I* do, I care."

I looked at him in bewilderment. "*You* do!"

"Yes, I do."

"But Sandy," I said in astonishment, "You . . ."

"Yes," he said in a wretched voice, "yes, I know." Following the train of my thoughts he turned round to face me, "There was all that in the barn, I know about that, I've never stopped thinking about it, wishing I'd never done it, but Katie, it wasn't *personal*, it wasn't done to hurt *you*, it was done out of spite, it was . . ."

". . . against Oliver." I nodded. "I knew that."

"The thing was, he was so *bloody* . . ."

". . . Yes."

"And he never bloody well . . ."

". . . Noticed."

"No."

"I do understand."

"Katie," he said desperately, "don't go with him, *don't*."

"I have to," I said. "He's all I've got. I love him."

He looked at me for a moment, then turned back to the middleweight. I watched as he cut out the next few plaits with a deadly concentration. The middleweight stretched his neck, arching it, glad to be free from the restraint.

"Goodbye Sandy," I said. "I have to go. People are waiting."

"Oh, he said. He rubbed his hands through the crinkled hair, massaging the roots, "you're off now then, are you?" His attitude had completely changed. He might hardly have known me. "Just one thing then, before you go."

Oh," I said cautiously, "what's that?"

"The next time he kicks you in the bloody teeth, remember you can always cry on my shoulder," he said.

SIXTEEN

In this way I had gone to work for The Count, in his immaculate, but small, purpose-built stable yard beside his beautiful, but typically extravagant Regency house with its balconies, its balustrading, and its formal garden overflowing with urns and statuary.

Dressage at its most advanced level, High School, as it is called, is not a sport, it is quite definitely art, and like art, can be regarded either as an essentially cultured form of recreational activity, or as a rather expensive indulgence. This fact alone tends to set dressage apart from, some would say above, the rest of the horse world; and, of course, because there is precious little in the way of financial reward in dressage, a horse takes many years to train and its eventual value on the open market would by no means repay the hours of training involved, this guarantees its exclusivity to some extent. Thus, the appeal of dressage is limited to a rather specific person, probably best typified by the artistic, dedicated equine aesthete, preferably with time and money at his disposal.

The Count had no more than ten or twelve horses in his yard at one time; ten when I arrived. These comprised an advanced horse which would be ridden only by Oliver or the Count himself, two horses at intermediate standard, one of which was at livery, three novices, two of them in the Count's ownership, and the rest young horses at various stages in their training, one of which was unbroken.

The horses were educated in the classical tradition, following closely upon the basic training methods of the Spanish Riding School, where the art of equestrianism has been developed to its highest form. Though not Lipizzaner, true to the Lipizzaner principle, they were not broken until their fourth year, and their education progressed very slowly and with great thoroughness.

The first year was devoted entirely to introducing the horse to the saddle and bridle, the lunge, and the rider, with the aim of establishing a mutual confidence and to teach him to go straight and forward. In the second year, correct contact with the bit was established, and work on the circle and towards collection would increase balance, suppleness and muscle development. In the third year there was extension and lateral work, where the horse was taught to move not only forwards, but sideways at the same time, and the *volte* (a tight circle) and the rein-back would be introduced. Finally, in the fourth year, and this only if the horse had progressed satisfactorily in the previous years and achieved its potential, training in the more advanced movements such as the flying change, the counter canter (i.e. cantering to the left with the right leg leading), the *pirouette*, and the *piaffe* and *passage* would begin.

The ultimate movements of High School, the so-called 'airs above the ground' were not performed in the Count's establishment. Surprisingly, because extravagance was in his very nature, he was scornful of them and considered them to be of no value whatsoever, maintaining that when the art of High School had reached its zenith in the sixteenth century, there had been sound reasoning behind the teaching of such equine acrobatics as the *levade*, the *croupade* and the *courbette*, because when performed in battle, they could save the cavalryman and his mount from the sword, the axe and the spear. Today however, he saw no sound reason to perform such movements, seeing no particular beauty in their execution and nothing beneficial in their attainment. Dressage to Count Von Der Drehler was totally concerned with developing the gaits of the horse to their fullest extent. The 'airs above the ground', viewed in this context, were totally superfluous.

It was my job to look after the youngest horses in the stable and I was given the task of training the unbroken four-year-old under the personal supervision of the Count himself. I was soon totally engrossed and involved in this, working to establish a trust and basic discipline, introducing him (there were no mares in the yard, the Count considered them too emotional) to the saddle and bridle which was always first fitted in the familiar confines of the stable, and by degrees to the cavesson, the lunge rein, and thence to work on the lunge itself. I was relieved to find that this was not all that different to what I had been doing in the Ensdale yard, and that preparing horses for the show ring had been a good training because I had already learned to be meticulous, to appreciate that no detail was small enough to be unimportant, and I was also gratified to find that I had been taught to lunge well because the Count was very strict about the way his horses were lunged, insisting that careless lunging could ruin a horse before anyone had even set foot to stirrup.

It was pleasant and rewarding work, particularly as the horses I was working with had been selected with regard to their intelligence, conformation and equable temperament – what the horse actually thinks about performing dressage we do not know and will never properly discover, but in order to perform well, he must look as though he is enjoying himself, and no unwilling horse could ever excell in such a discipline.

As my young horses were never worked for more than two half-hour sessions per day, I soon found myself being drawn into other activities in the establishment. One moment I might find myself assisting from the ground when one of the horses in its fourth year of training was being taught the *piaffe*, where he is required to spring from one diagonal to the other as if he is trotting on the spot; the next I might be called upon to lunge one of the riders who came for training, sending the horse trotting and cantering round whilst the rider performed suppling exercises without the benefit of reins or stirrups in order that the seat should become deep and strong and the hands and legs controlled enough to apply the aids precisely and independently. Eventually it was suggested that I embark upon several months of these lunge lessons myself, so that I should be able to join in the training sessions with the Count, and this I readily agreed to do. Not only was I engrossed and involved in my work, I was now intoxicated and entranced by the art of dressage.

I knew already, of course, that the Count was a brilliant instructor. Watching him at work with his disciples, I could see that he was everything one could possibly desire and expect in a tutor. In turn he could be intimidating, theatrical, joyful, fierce, demanding and amusing, but he was never less than illuminating, and always inspiring, uplifting his pupils so they could astonish even themselves with their newly discovered ability. I immediately understood why he commanded such reverence, and why Oliver had determined to come here. And Oliver was good value. He was an outstanding pupil and the Count was proud of him, using him as an example to his pupils, as a showpiece to demonstrate movements to his classes, as the leading rider in his displays, as well as adopting him as his companion and confidante.

Nor was the Count indifferent to me. He was so unfailingly kind and instructive, so genuinely interested in my welfare, and so anxious that I should further my education in horsemanship, that gradually I grew very fond of him, and I believe he was fond of me.

One afternoon, I sat at his side in the small observer's gallery of the indoor manège watching Oliver riding on the tan below. The horse was a seven-year-old black entire – black seemed to be a colour much favoured by the Count, unless it was just coincidence that the most promising horses he came across happened to be that colour. Fully developed and muscled, the horse Oliver rode was a magnificently powerful animal, emanating intelligence and vitality.

Oliver had been teaching the *pirouette*, a turn at the canter in which the inner hind leg turns on the spot whilst the forelegs describe a bounding arc around the hindquarters. Count Von Der Drehler always insisted that his horses should be taught the *pirouette* from the canter in *renvers* (a lateral movement where the horse continues to move forward but with his forehand bent to the outside) on the square away from the walls, according to the method laid down by the classical riding master of France, Francois Robichon de La Gueriniere, believing that it made it easier for the horse to understand what was expected of him, but it was still a difficult movement to execute correctly, demanding enormous control and concentration from both horse and rider. Oliver had been working the black entire for a month on this movement alone, and was now to demonstrate the horse's progress by performing a *passade* (a very small turn in a *half-volte* where the hindquarters move a smaller circle than the forehand), and *renvers* with a *pirouette.*

The Count watched the horse intently as Oliver performed some lateral movements and *voltes* to assure himself of the entire's attention, suppleness and obedience when;

"You do realise, Kathryn," he said somewhat unexpectedly, "that your brother, Oliver is brilliantly gifted, that he is quite out of the ordinary, really most exceptional?"

"Yes," I said, "of course I realise it." I glanced at him, wondering why he had thought to point it out when he knew perfectly well that I realised it. Today, a deep yellow silk scarf enlivened the anciently tailored melton jacket, waisted and skirted, that the Count wore above his habitual black breeches and boots. A rose of similar hue bloomed in his buttonhole.

"I do not know what he will achieve. Even I cannot set a limit to the development of his talent."

He looked at me with the bright shrewd, deeply-set brown eyes that more than anything about him betrayed his foreign descent.

"But I am aware that I have given him all the knowledge that I can give. I know, Kathryn, and I believe he knows," he said, "that he will gain no more from me."

In silence we watched the black entire execute a perfect three-quarter *pirouette* through two corners of the manège, and pass the third in *renvers*. I did not reply to the Count. I was not sure what I should say. Below us, the black horse straightened and made a flying change, with Oliver's disciplined legs at his sides, with his controlling hands on the reins.

"He will need to go abroad very soon. If he is to maintain his progress, it is essential that he widens his experience. He should go to Germany, to France and to Vienna, perhaps to Sweden. There is always something to be learned from people who practise the same form of art."

Down in the manège the entire was performing *half-pirouettes* to the outside of the circle. Oliver's face was rapt with an immense concentration. Nobody, nothing existed for him apart from the black horse between his thighs.

"In this country, you see, Kathryn," the Count went on, "we are too new to dressage. Your ancestors preferred the thrills of the chase and the racetrack, to the more academic pleasures of the High School. There is not the tradition here, there is not the depth of knowledge. There are not enough sufficiently knowledgeable and practised instructors. There are not even the horses . . ."

"What are you trying to tell me?" I kept my eyes on the black horse, on the black bandaged legs as they rose and fell with impeccable rhythm. Of course, I already knew what he was endeavouring in his tactful and intelligent manner, to convey. Oliver was planning to leave him. I felt despair begin to gather in my chest. Oliver had said nothing of this to me. And yet had I really imagined that he would stay with the Count for ever? When his knowledge had been utilised, exhausted, just as Charity Ensdale's had been, had I thought he would chose to stay on, out of gratitude perhaps, out of compassion? Of course he would not. Oliver was not like that.

My eyes followed the black horse as he cantered onto the circle, was asked for a transition to trot, as he moved into walk and was allowed a loose rein. Now that the demonstration was over, Oliver leaned forward over the gleaming shoulder and rubbed the hard, muscled neck with his knuckles. He had not mentioned his plans to me. For all my hard work, for all my loyalty and my absolute faithfulness, he had not even granted me this and as I watched him reward the entire with love and caresses and grateful words, I was numbed by his treachery.

"What I am saying is that offers have been made for him already," the Count said. "I have not been informed of this, you understand, not by Oliver, at least. He has not chosen to discuss it with me, but I am not a fool, I am aware of what goes on. I do know that offers have been made, and that so far they have been refused, but once the seed is sown and the soil is fertile, then it is only a matter of time. I am right, Kathryn, am I not, in my suspicion that none of these offers have been mentioned to you?"

"You are right," I managed to say, "nothing has been said. Oliver has not told me anything."

Below us, Oliver had halted the entire and he looked up towards the gallery enquiringly. The Count waved a hand to him in gratified acknowledgment of training meticulously accomplished, of movements impeccably executed. Oliver smiled and raised his whip in a salute before turning the black horse away.

Count Von Der Drehler sighed.

"It is as I expected. But you should know, Kathryn, that one day soon there will be an offer made that he cannot refuse. I know this is so because I have seen it happen before, and with people of far less talent than your brother. I am telling you this now, I am warning you, so that you may be prepared for it when it happens, so that you will have considered your own future and will know which direction to take, because it *will* happen. Oliver will leave soon. I am certain of it."

I stared down into the manège, not seeing anything, feeling devastated. It was a terrible shock to me to learn that my life was about to be turned upside down again and that I was powerless to do anything about it. I knew the Count had been right to tell me, and I also knew he was right to infer that it was time I started to plan my own life, to move out of Oliver's shadow. And yet I was not sure that I could. Oliver was all I had. I needed him, and I wanted to believe that in his own way, he needed me. But was I fooling myself? And what of the Count? How did he feel about Oliver's departure? Here was someone who also loved him, who had given much, and now had nothing more to give, and yet was wise enough and noble enough to allow that it was both inevitable and right that Oliver should leave in order to further his own ends.

"And when it happens, when he does leave," I asked him, "what about you? Will you mind?"

From below, like the distant thunder of an

approaching storm, came the rumble of the sliding doors as they opened to allow Oliver and the black entire to leave the manège.

"When he leaves," the Count said, rising from his seat and turning away from me in order to retrieve his stick, so that I was unable to see the expression on his face, "I believe I shall mind more than I have minded anything in the whole of my life."

SEVENTEEN

The solution came from Francesca. A few weeks later I received a letter informing me that she had passed her preliminary examinations and was coming back to organise the opening of her riding school within the month. Reminding me of my promise, she asked if I was still willing to help her. I replied that I was.

So when Oliver eventually told me that he had accepted a position at *Reinstitut von Neindorff* in West Germany, I was both resigned and prepared for it, but what I had not expected was to be asked to go with him. The position offered was that of a groom, and a backward step, but even so, had the news taken me unawares I would probably have agreed to it for Oliver's sake. As it was I had no choice but to refuse, having given my word to Francesca.

Oliver tried hard to persuade me to change my mind and took my refusal badly. In anger he accused me of selfishness and of deceit.

". . . Making your arrangements with Francesca, without a thought to how I might feel about it, making promises without informing me, without regard for any plans I might have made," he had said angrily.

"And what about you," I had countered, "did you think about me when you were making your arrangements? Did you consider my feelings as you were planning to leave? No, you did not! If you had any consideration at all for me, you would have told me you were leaving *months* ago!

"How could I have told you months ago," he had demanded furiously, "when I have only just decided to accept the offer made to me? How could I tell you something I did not know myself?"

Ah, I had thought, but you did know, didn't you, Oliver? You had received offers long before the one you finally accepted. You had already decided to leave. But out of loyalty to the Count I held my tongue. I kept my silence, I did not betray his confidence. And in this way we parted, with bitterness on Oliver's side and sadness on mine. I wrote to him often at first, but as the only replies I received were in the form of postcards, and the only message they bore was a mere signature, gradually my letters became less frequent, and finally I saw no point in writing at all. During the next four years I was to receive postcards from such various places as Karlsruhe, Etampes, Saumur, Munster, Stromsholm, Helsingborg, Barthus, Avessada, Vienna, and Jerez de la Frontera. Few of these names meant anything to me at all. On my birthday and at Christmas I received conventional greetings cards. These also bore nothing apart from the usual unaccompanied signature – *Oliver.*

Until Francesca returned, I stayed on with the Count. He had invited me to continue working at his establishment, but whilst I was grateful for his offer, I knew I must get away, if only to leave behind the things which reminded me daily of Oliver. If in some way I had to begin to build a career for myself, if I was to be alone now, it could not be in a place where Oliver had been before me, I had to start afresh. I did not know how I should like working with Francesca, I had no experience of teaching children to ride, but two years ago I had made a faithful promise, and now that it had been reaffirmed I had to honour that promise and I was determined to do so.

If any other reason for leaving the Count's establishment was needed it came soon enough in the form of another young boy, slim and golden-haired, with a gentle manner and a graceful seat in the saddle. I had watched him working the horses under the Count's instruction and thought him malleable and promising, if somewhat lacking in character, and without the edge of steel necessary for success in such a disciplined art. I could see that there was a resemblance to Oliver, but he was a pale shadow, inferior in every way. He was beautiful, like Oliver, but he did not have the easy, sensuous look that Oliver had in the saddle, he did not have his cool elegance, nor his level, rather challenging gaze, he lacked the glamour, the slight air of ruthlessness, all of which drew eyes wherever he went. Oliver had changed a lot since our gymkhana days, and in comparison, the golden-haired boy was a child. But there was no doubt that he was a pleasure to watch in the manège, and his gentle approach was appreciated by some of the horses, although I never saw him ride the black entire

I was soon to notice that the boy appeared increasingly often in the manège, and would often be seen walking round the yard a few steps behind the Count, carrying his coat perhaps, or his stick, but it was only when I glimpsed him sitting in the back of the car with Count Von Der Drehler as it left the yard one morning, that I properly realised that here was the latest protegé, the replacement for Oliver, and I could not endure the thought of it.

I could not bear to watch someone else leading the displays, helping to demonstrate movements to a class of pupils, riding the horses that Oliver had ridden. I made myself absent. I stayed away. I did not blame the Count. I was glad for him, and when I left it was possible to shed tears of genuine regret, but it was with a feeling of relief that I walked out of the establishment for the last time.

Francesca, meanwhile, had encountered an unexpected obstacle when the Diocese had forbidden the use of church land for the purpose of running a business for commercial gain. This meant she had to look elsewhere for land with suitable buildings at an affordable rent, and this was proving an impossible task. Everywhere she looked, the rent had been beyond her means until finally, just as she had been about to abandon the project altogether, she had been offered Pond Cottage, its buildings, and its waterlogged acres, at a comparatively modest monthly rental and without any tenancy agreement or capital sum in advance. She accepted it, and in this way began her running battle with the decrepit stabling, the woefully neglected cottage, and the constant problems arising from the flooding of the river. It seemed to me a grossly unfair trick of fate when I learned much later that the river that so precisely and evenly watered Oliver's luxuriant acres, was the very same that ruined Francesca's by its over generosity.

In the years that I spent with Francesca, I was never convinced that I really enjoyed riding school work. The surroundings did not help, but I was never engrossed and totally involved the way I had been with the show horses, or with the training of my young horses at the Count's establishment. There had been times when I had thought to leave, to do something else, but Francesca needed me, and perhaps above all things, I wanted someone to need me, and so I stayed, and I endured.

I did not forget Oliver. Every week, every month, I combed the horse papers and the glossy magazines for news of him. Spasmodically, short paragraphs would appear reporting upon his successes in international competition. From *Horse and Hound* I first learned that he had given up competition and turned professional, and then came the issue which carried his photograph on the cover, and inside, the news that he had landed the richest sponsorship in the history of any branch of equestrian sport, and that after a short period in Spain, where he was engaged in selecting staff and Andalusian horses, he would be returning to England to open a training establishment of his own.

The next postcard I received was from Cazallo, and this time there had been more than just a signature, there had been an offer of the position as Oliver's personal assistant when he returned, and with it, or so I had imagined, forgiveness. In the face of Francesca's disapproval and indignation, I had accepted, my own delight and relief at the prospect of being reunited with Oliver eclipsing any concern I might otherwise have had for how she might feel, and how she might manage when I had gone.

Well, I had not lasted long with the Oliver who had returned. Four years as a prima donna in the dressage centres of Europe had turned him into a stranger and I had found that I no longer knew him.

But now, stranger or not, there was only Oliver left who could help St. Luke, and it was I who had to ask him. And this evening, with Francesca absent for a few hours, was the perfect time. I steeled myself to do it. I picked up the telephone.

As I expected, John Englehart's voice answered. Trying to sound confident, as if I was sure he would want to speak to me, I asked if I could be put through to the house, to Oliver.

There was an uncertain silence, before the well-trained voice said: "Oliver Jasny does not accept personal calls. This is his secretary speaking, can I ask what this is about?"

I might have realised it would not be that easy. It would take a wily bird to slip past John Englehart's ardent vigilance.

"John," I said, "this is Kathryn. I need to speak to Oliver rather urgently. Is he there?"

"Kathryn . . ." Now that he realised who he was speaking to, the assured telephone manner faltered.

"He is *there,* isn't he?" I felt sure he must be. I knew he very rarely left the premises in the evenings.

"He is, but you can't speak to him. He . . . he isn't available."

I was not to be forestalled as easily as that. "Now look here, John, I said firmly, "I need to speak to Oliver, and I intend to speak to him. This is urgent, it is a family matter."

Even this approach did not have the desired effect. "He can't *speak* to you, Kathryn," he insisted, "he's engaged, he has a . . . an evening lesson."

I knew him to be a poor liar, and I knew he was lying now although I did not know why. Could Oliver have given instructions that I was to be turned away if I ever tried to approach him again? Would he have done that? I knew him capable of it, and I had said some unforgivable things when we had parted. And yet I did not believe that this was the reason. John Englehart was more than usually nervous. If he had been carrying out Oliver's instructions he would have sounded more confident. With Oliver's authority behind him, he would have found the courage to be firm. But he was not. For some reason, John Englehart was frightened.

"Is something wrong?" I asked him, "Has something happened?"

"Well, there has been a . . ." he hesitated, as if uncertain whether to proceed, but then it all came spilling out in a rush. "The thing is, Kathryn, there's been a bit of trouble with one of the caballerizos. He's always been a bit of a . . . well, Oliver's *never* liked him, and in the stable he's known to be *particularly* . . . He's just *rough* with the horses, and you know Oliver, he won't stand for that. I mean people don't matter to him all that much, but the *horses* . . . well, what happened was that he caught him at it, Oliver did. He was just walking past the stable, and there was a set to, he was really *vicious*, he beat him . . ."

"The caballerizo beat Oliver?" I could not imagine it.

"No, Oliver beat *him*, and now he's taken it to the tribunal, and he's tried to get Oliver for assault. I suppose the sponsors had to *know* about it, and now they're all involved . . . you wouldn't believe, Kathryn what a business it is."

I could believe it only too well. "But if he was ill-treating the *horses*..." I said

"Yes, but Oliver, he didn't half... the caballerizo was properly roughed up. I mean more than a *bit*, he had to be taken to hospital, he really *thrashed* him."

This was an entirely new development as far as I was concerned. I did not like the sound of it.

"So there's a sponsor's meeting going on, not an evening lesson at all?"

"Yes, we've got the police, the sponsor's, the union, and even somebody from the Spanish Embassy here." Already regretting his indiscretion, he added in a fraught tone, "Kathryn, you won't *tell* Oliver I told you all this? If he knew I'd discussed it, if he thought I'd told *anyone* about it, he'd cut my tongue out."

I thought this was probably true, and from our opposite ends of the telephone there was an uneasy silence whilst John Englehart struggled with his guilt, and I began to absorb fully the implications of what I had heard. In turn I was alarmed, appalled, and dismayed. I had even forgotten the original purpose of my telephone call. St. Luke and his problems were now far from my thoughts, which were now entirely directed towards Oliver and his predicament. I did not think there was anything I could usefully do to help. I could not get to the Training Centre because I had no transport. Only one bus a day connected us, and that left in the early morning and returned in the evening. And what would my presence achieve? Even if I were to saddle up one of the horses and ride the nine or so miles across country, what kind of reception could I expect? Would Oliver thank me for it? I did not think he would. There seemed nothing I could do other than to remind my brother that I existed, to let him know that if he needed me, I was available.

"John," I said, "I doubt if he will want to speak to me, but if you have an opportunity later, will you mention that I rang? Will you tell him that if he would like to ring me, I am on Cuckfield 272, and will be here for the rest of the evening?"

"Yes. Yes . . . all right," I heard him rustling about amongst his papers trying to find something to write with, ". . . Cuckfield 272. I will *tell* him, Kathryn, but you do understand I can't *promise* he'll ring, he'll make up his own mind about that, so don't blame me if he doesn't," I imagined him pushing back the mat of soft, spaniel hair, "you know how it is . . . you know *Oliver.*"

As a matter of fact, you are wrong, I thought as I replaced the receiver, that's just the trouble. I no longer know Oliver at all.

I sat by the telephone all evening, waiting for it to ring. Half of me knew it would not, the other half hoped that it would. When Francesca returned, looking exuberant and promisingly flushed, I could not bring myself to talk to her about it. I said nothing. I forced myself to move away from the telephone, to admit to myself that he was not going to call. Francesca had flounced through the door in the red and white dress and hurled herself across the lumpy, uncut moquette settee, purchased, like most of her furniture, from the House Clearance Centre in the nearest town, whilst St. Luke had been quietly divesting the vicarage of what should have been her's, in aid of St. Chad's. An air of triumph radiated out from her.

"Well," I asked, "how did it go?"

Tossing back the renaissance fringe, Francesca grinned

at me. The grey-green eyes sparkled with intrigue.

"I think it would be true to say," she said, "that it went very well indeed."

I was not in the mood for badinage. "Oh," I said shortly, "good."

"We had dinner," Francesca said, "no," she corrected herself, "first we had cocktails, *then* we had dinner . . ."

"Cocktails," I said, "how nice." My eyes strayed to the telephone. In my imagination I saw the caballerizo being carried out of the stable on a stretcher, and my blood was chilled by the thought of it.

"After that," Francesca continued, "we had coffee and brandy and chocolate orange peel."

I had never heard of chocolate orange peel, it sounded very exotic, but I could not tear my eyes away from the telephone. I heard John Englehart's voice saying . . . "People don't matter to him all that much," and I could see Oliver's face, cold and uncaring, and was suddenly desperately afraid for him.

"Then," Francesca said gleefully, "came the champagne."

Champagne! Despite my anxiety over Oliver, I looked at Francesca in surprise. "*Champagne!*" I said.

Francesca sat up properly on the settee and looked at me in a sober manner. "But that was after we had discussed the matter of Moor Park Stables," she said.

"Moor Park Stables?" Giving her the benefit of my fullest attention now, I stared. "Did you say *Moor Park Stables?*"

"I did," Francesca confirmed. "And I am sure you would like to know that we will be moving out of here and into the yard there, just as soon as the stable flat has been refurbished."

"*What?*"

"Of course, I didn't agree to it immediately," she went on, smoothing the red and white dress calmly over her knees, "it wouldn't have been quite the thing to have appeared *too* keen, and I still have to give our definite answer. I only agreed that we would consider it."

I dropped down onto the arm of the settee and stared at her in disbelief. "You did WHAT?"

The grey-green eyes regarded me in an artless manner. "But I could hardly say yes straight away, could I? I have to be in a position to strike a bargain, otherwise I shall be at a disadvantage. The rent he is asking is more than we are paying now and I hope to persuade him to reduce it. Of course, I do believe," Francesca said, "that Moor Park does have certain advantages."

The telephone shrilled. As she was sitting next to it, she picked up the receiver.

"Cuckfield 272 . . . No, really, I haven't been disturbed . . . Yes, Kathryn is here . . . No, honestly, it's no trouble at all, she's practically by my side, I'm not in the least inconvenienced." She held out the receiver. "A call for you," she said.

"I do believe I have just been speaking to Francesca," Oliver's voice said.

"Yes." I had not yet recovered from Francesca's bombshell, and now I was further amazed to receive his call. I did not know what to say.

"I suppose it would have been polite to have told her to whom she was speaking, but I was rather afraid she would replace the receiver," Oliver said.

Francesca was following the conversation with a lively interest. "It's Oliver," I told her. "He would have told you, but felt you would have cut him off."

She looked at me, wide-eyed. "Well, yes," she admitted in a stunned way, "I suppose I might have."

"I told Francesca, she says she probably would have."

"Rather fortunate then, that I did not introduce myself," Oliver said in a dry voice. I was relieved to hear him sounding so cool and composed. If he was in trouble, his voice gave nothing away.

"I tried to ring you earlier," I told him, "but I was told you were not available."

"No, I had a pressing engagement."

I could almost have smiled at such a masterful understatement. "So I heard."

There was an ominous silence. I had not intended to betray John Englehart's indiscretion, and I hoped that I had not done so by the tone of my voice. I felt it was useless to try to say more on the telephone, not even about St. Luke, especially with Francesca staring at me incredulously, hanging onto my every word.

"Oliver, I wondered . . . please, if I could come and see you. I need to ask you something, but I can't really talk about it now, it isn't really convenient."

"But of course," Oliver said, "I will see you whenever you wish. When would you like to come?"

Somewhat taken aback by his readiness to comply, I blurted, "I don't know . . . I hadn't thought . . . whenever . . ."

"What about tomorrow," Oliver suggested, "I shall be free in the afternoon, at any time after four pm."

"That would be lovely," I said gratefully, "I'll come then."

"And I shall look forward to it." The line clicked. I

handed the receiver back to Francesca. She said in outrage, "You're not planning to ask *Oliver* for the five thousand pounds?"

"I might," I slid down on the settee, feeling totally drained and exhausted. An argument with Francesca was the very last thing I wanted.

"You do realise that he'll *refuse*?" she demanded.

I shrugged. Just at that moment I did not feel capable of realising anything.

"But when he does refuse," Francesca conceded angrily, "you may be sure it will be done with the utmost courtesy. He still has the most beautiful manners."

She banged the receiver back into its cradle, her previous mood of triumphant self-congratulation quite banished.

"He always was a smooth *bastard*."

EIGHTEEN

I arrived early for my appointment with Oliver, he was still engaged in a lesson, although the main part of it, the instruction, was over. Oliver worked his pupils hard, but never for more than forty-five minutes at a stretch believing that this was the maximum time he could demand their total concentration.

I climbed the steps through the public gallery, empty but for a group of perhaps six or eight people, grooms probably, to the horses in the manège below, and went into the commentary box to wait. Through the glass partition I looked down at the horses, watching them cantering to the familiar strains of Beethoven's *Für Elise*, the soft thud of their hooves falling exactly three beats to the bar. The Training Centre seemed a far cry from the Pond Cottage Riding School. Both establishments were concerned with the teaching of horsemanship, and yet, I couldn't help thinking, how great is the gulf between the grass roots of equitation and the rarefied atmosphere of dressage.

John Englehart was sitting at the table, surrounded by piles of papers and cassette tapes, talking in agonised tones to someone on the telephone.

"But this has nothing to do with whether they are good plants, or bad plants," he was saying desperately. "Petunias, he suggested, or fuchsias, even salvia's at a pinch, but *not* geraniums, he won't have them on the place, he says the smell makes him sick . . . . . . Yes, I *told* you, he wants them *all* out, the tubs, the troughs, the windowboxes, and the border by the house . . . . . Well, yes I know he did, and I'm sorry about that, I'm sure he didn't mean to upset the lad really, but there must be someone else you can send . . . . Yes, I *do* mean straight away!"

The receiver slammed down. As I turned, the spaniel eyes fixed upon me accusingly,

"Kathryn, you needn't have told him," he said in a distraught voice, "You'd never *believe* the names he called me this morning!"

So Oliver had guessed that I knew. I might have known that he would.

"I only said I'd been told he had a pressing engagement," I said defensively, "I didn't say anything else at all."

"It wasn't *what* you said, it was the way you said it. 'So I *heard*,' you said, in such a way that he just couldn't doubt that you knew!"

"Oh, John, I'm sorry if I got you into trouble," I said, "but believe me, it was not intentional, it was just a stupid slip of the tongue. And anyway," I looked at him with suspicion, "how do you know exactly what was said?"

"Oliver told me."

"Oh, no he did not!" He was lying again, I could tell. "You make it your business to know everything about Oliver, don't you?" I said, "You watch his every movement, you read all his letters, even his personal ones, and when he rang me last night, I expect you were eavesdropping in your habitual manner on the office switchboard!"

"Kathryn, I don't know how you could even *suggest* such a thing!" The tone was outraged, but the spaniel eyes moved anxiously towards the manège, as if Oliver, by some super-human faculty, might somehow be empowered to overhear our conversation.

"You shouldn't do it, John," I warned, "you will be found out one of these days." A red light winked on the control panel. John Englehart reached out a finger to press the button which operated the sliding doors.

"I don't know why I stay with him, anyway," he said in a sulky voice, "he's a monster, that's what he is."

But a monster you can't live without, I thought as I watched Oliver leave the manège by the rear personnel door. And you will never find the strength to walk away either, you will just go on watching, and listening, and hoping, and you will always be wretched, you will always be lonely, because Oliver will never notice you. You are no more to him than a stray dog, to throw a crust to, or to kick out of his way, but never allow into the house.

As I ran down the gallery steps, John Englehart's voice floated out over the public address system.

"The music will continue for ten minutes after the doors have opened for the benefit of anyone who wishes to continue . . ." His voice, never wholly steady, faltered noticeably. I could see that the job was too much for him, that he was struggling to cope, hoping that Oliver would not notice. I knew however, that Oliver would notice, and I wondered how long he would tolerate it.

Out in the yard, Oliver waited, leaning over a half door. In his dressage breeches, his slim brown boots, and his silk shirt, he looked not quite real to me, he could have been a glamorised horseman, brought on solely for the benefit of the cameras, to be ushered away afterwards, when there was dirty work to be done.

He smiled at me and opened the stable door. I had not expected this whole-hearted forgiveness, and was made cautious by it. I did not trust him. Inside the stable, one of the dark-eyed Spanish caballerizos was strapping at San Domingo's hard, gleaming coat. The Andalusian horse is nearly always grey, occasionally black, and San Domingo was unusual because of his colour, a strong liver chestnut, flecked with grey. As we entered, the horse fixed its large, intelligent eyes upon Oliver, and whickered an affectionate greeting, but the caballerizo stopped work abruptly, grabbed up his equipment in a panic striken way, and would have bolted out into the yard had Oliver not caught him by the collar of his shirt.

"Rugs, dear boy," he said, "before you leave us."

The caballerizo replaced the horse's undersheet, and placed on top of it the cream day rug with its double bound border of blue and ruby, and the *Tio Fino* insignia in the corner. His fingers shook uncontrollably as he pushed the straps through the buckles and keepers on the iron-arch roller, and he left the stable with obvious relief.

"Oliver," I said, "he was terrified of you."

"So he should be. I'm a boy beater, haven't you heard?"

"Well, I . . ."

"I feel sure you were supplied with every detail by our

voluble friend, Mr. Englehart, but I assure you that it will go no further." he said, "And you need have no fears on my behalf," he added, "the sponsor's have agreed to pay the unfortunate boy off most handsomely."

"But they won't do it again, Oliver. You will have to be careful."

"I shall be." He leaned against the Andalusian's big, powerful shoulder and looked at me with cool amusement. "Am I right to suppose that life in the swamp with Francesca has proved intolerable?"

Loyalty to Francesca prevented me from saying how intolerable I had found it. "It isn't all that bad."

"But you have decided to accept my offer to come here as second rider?"

"No, that isn't why I came."

"It isn't?" I fancied the temperature dropped by several degrees, but I may have imagined it. With his hands in the pockets of his breeches, and his shoulderblades resting on the horse's forearm, he raised an eyebrow enquiringly.

I saw no point in beating about the bush.

"I've come to ask you to help St. Luke," I said, "he needs five thousand pounds."

Abruptly, Oliver straightened. Astonishment appeared in the dark-fringed blue eyes, followed by stark incredulity.

"Explain to me, Kathryn, why I should give St. Luke five thousand pounds," he exclaimed, "and perhaps more to the point, from where I should obtain it?"

"Well," I began "I rather thought . . ."

"You rather thought that I had means at my disposal, that I was wealthy," he said in an exasperated voice. "Like many other people, you assume that because I have the trappings, I also have unlimited funds into which I can dip my hand and scatter for the benefit of all and sundry!"

"St. Luke is not all and sundry," I said, stung.

"Kathryn, I have no money," Oliver said, "for St. Luke or for anyone else."

"You misunderstand me," I said. "If... if you would just let me *explain* .."

"Everything you see here belongs to *Tio Fino*, everything," Oliver emphasized, "this stable, this horse, the straw beneath our feet. If everything the sponsors have supplied were to be taken away this very second, I would be left with nothing apart from the clothes upon my back, and even they," he said with bitterness, "have been bought with Spanish money. You *know* how it is with me, I have never had access to private means. I am as totally dependent upon my sponsors now, as I ever was upon the generosity of my patrons."

I turned away from him in resignation. I could see that it was futile to pursue the matter if he would not allow me to speak.

"I hardly need to be reminded by what means you have achieved your success," I said.

There was an arctic silence.

"That was an exceedingly uncalled for remark," Oliver said in a cold voice.

I went to the door and, reaching over it, drew back the bolt.

"I have whipped people for less."

I did not doubt it. I pushed the door. It swung open.

"But even I, who have achieved my success by improper and disgraceful means, am prepared to listen, if it is true that I have misunderstood you," Oliver said.

I looked round at him. One arm was casually slung across San Domingo's strongly crested neck, and with the fingers of the other hand he was gently stroking the loose, velvety flesh beneath the Andalusian's jowl.

"I am aware that I have *some* obligation to St. Luke," he said, "and by whatever standards you judge me, Kathryn, you cannot deny that I have always fulfilled my obligations in whatever form they may have been."

I stood in the doorway, staring back into the stable to where he stood with the horse. They say horses are not capable of love, but the Andalusian loved Oliver, you had only to see the way it looked at him to know it.

"Oliver," I said, "I was not going to ask that you give St. Luke five thousand pounds, not just like that, I was going to ask if there was a possibility that you could stage a display, a demonstration, in aid of St. Chad's. If the roof isn't repaired, if the money isn't found, the Diocese are going to force a closure. They are going to move St. Luke from the Vicarage into a modern bungalow near St. Aidan's. It will break his heart. He has managed to raise half the money by selling the furniture, furniture that by rights should be left to Francesca, but soon there will be nothing left to sell. I came to ask you because I thought . . . I thought . . ."

Oliver stared at me. "Close the *church*?" he said.

"Yes."

"Move St. Luke out of the *Vicarage*?"

I nodded.

"Over my dead *body*," he said.

NINETEEN

I wanted to go and visit St. Luke, to let him know that we were doing something positive, to give him hope, but the summer holidays had just begun, the children were home from school, and Pond Cottage Riding School was fully booked every day. Francesca and I were giving lessons from eight in the morning until eight in the evening, and after that there were the horses to attend to, and the tack to clean. I found it exhausting and tedious, but I knew that we had to take the money when we could, and that we should only gain a respite when it rained. There was no sign of rain. The sky was cloudless, the sun blazed down, the mud dried, the first brave shoots of new grass withered and scorched, and the ground began to crack open. But the pupils flooded in and their money filled the corn bins and the barn, paid for the farrier and for a lorry of chippings to soften the ground in the manège.

In my infrequent spare moments I tried to ring the Vicarage, but whatever time it happened to be, it seemed that St. Luke was absent. In the end I decided to ring Mrs. Fernley and ask if she would mind calling in with a message.

"Well, of course I can pop across to the Vicarage for

you, Kathryn," she said, "I know just what it's like trying to catch a hold of the Reverend, slippery as soap he is to get a grip on, up and down the village all day long and everybody running after him in all directions, especially this week with the fête on."

"Oh, of *course*." I had forgotten about the fête. This was good news, because with the fête to occupy him, St. Luke would be far too busy to organise the disposal of any more furniture.

"I don't suppose there is any point in asking him to ring me, because he will only forget," I said. "But could you possibly tell him something for me, or leave him a note?"

"I can leave a note on the hall table for him this morning, Kathryn," she said. "I can pop it in on my way to the butcher. If you can just stay there a minute, whilst I get my pencil . . ."

There was a crash as the receiver went down, and a short interval before it was taken up again.

"Now what is it you want to say, dear? You just tell me nice and slowly and I'll write it down."

There was some fumbling as the telephone receiver and the pencil changed hands.

"Oliver . . . has . . . found . . . a . . . way . . . to . . . raise . . . the . . . money. Would that be young Master Oliver you're talking about? Well, I *never*. It must be nearly ten years since we've seen him in the village. He went abroad didn't he? I know that because he used to send postcards to the Vicarage now and again. He was such a lovely looking boy, such nice manners . . . Yes, you can go on, dear, Will . . . be . . . in . . . touch . . . soon . . . Kathryn. Is that all of it? There's nothing else you want to say? All right my love, you can leave it to me. I'll make sure the Reverend gets it!"

I put down the telephone. I tried to imagine St. Luke's face as he read the message and realised that St. Chad's was saved. For some reason I could not conjure up anything at all.

"Now, counting strides as you ride a large circle at a working trot, counting out loud, one-two, one-two, to establish the rhythm of the pace, taking care that the pony does not speed up or slow down, remembering that you must dictate the pace at all times . . . . circling round to approach the poles, bringing your pony, straight, and trotting down the poles, still counting, one-two, one-two-clunk – what did that tell you, Joanna?"

Joanna, releasing the reins so that the pony dropped into an undisciplined shambling walk as he approached the line of attendant pupils awaiting their turn, looked at me blankly.

"It tells me he's lazy," she hazarded, "or else his shoes are too big for his feet."

From the end of the line of poles, where she was positioned as a human marker in order to focus the children's attention forward instead of downwards onto the poles, Francesca's burst of laughter rang out.

"No, it tells you that Foggy can't quite reach the poles, set as they are, from that rather collected, shorter pace."

I could cheerfully have wrung the child's neck, but I swallowed my impatience and forced myself to be pleasant. I could not, dare not, allow myself to admit how much I detested riding school work.

"Next time, Joanna, ask for a slightly longer stride,

which means a little less collection, not quite such a short rein, a little more length to the neck, but no loss of impulsion."

As the child stared at me with total incomprehension, I turned back to the waiting line hastily. "Next please!"

The outside telephone bell shrilled. Francesca motioned that she would answer it and ran off towards the yard. Her arms and her face were deeply tanned and her hair, brightened by the sun, was plaited and wound around her head. Little puffs of dust rose from her rubber boots as she thudded across the baked paddock.

Davina, back at Pond Cottage after a voluntary absence of several weeks following the crow-scarer incident, rode the dun pony out of line and jabbed it into a trot with her heels. I had soon discovered that it was pointless to admonish the children for their lack of refinement in applying the aids, because it was the only way they could get the ponies to move. The average pony is not schooled to be sensitive to the leg, nor is the average child endowed with enough developed muscular co-ordination to apply sufficient leg pressure, or to drive their pelvic bones into the saddle. Nor is there any point in trying to attain these things too early given the insensitive, phlegmatic type of animal best suited to beginners and young children. It would have been both dangerous and unkind to subject a more responsive, schooled animal to the unconscious abuses of the inexperienced.

Francesca returned.

"It's Oliver, be quick. He's probably ringing about the demonstration – I'll take over this end until you get back."

As far as the arrangements for raising the money for St.

Luke were concerned, she was both hopeful and suspicious, wanting to believe that it would happen, but distrustful of the means, and if I had hoped to see her warm towards Oliver at last, then so far I had been disappointed.

I ran to the telephone in the tackroom. "Oliver?"

"You are out of breath, Kathryn," he observed, "I hope this is not inconvenient for you."

"Not at all," I gasped. Panting and scarlet-faced after my two-acre sprint, I imagined him in the office, leaning back on his chair with one immaculate boot on the desk, the fingers of his free hand playing idly with the deersfoot paperknife.

"I thought you would like to know that I have seen the sponsors and we are agreed in principle, although there are only three possible dates for the display; Tuesday the fourteenth of September, Friday the seventh of October, or Saturday the twenty-seventh of October."

"Oliver, how simply *marvellous*,, I can't tell you how . . ."

"I have arranged to perform a festival of dressage. My best pupils will ride a quadrille, and I will give a solo performance. I have asked for a quintet to play live chamber music and for the manège to be banked with flowers in cream and crimson and red. There will be a reception beforehand naturally, and afterwards, my stables will be open for inspection. In order to relieve people of such an astonishing amount of money," Oliver said, "I suppose I must allow myself to be a little inconvenienced."

I held onto the receiver, hardly able to speak.

"You must decide, of course, which is the most

convenient date, but I would point out that to stage the festival on a Saturday afternoon would bring the maximum amount of people, and if we are to reach our target, it is vitally important that every seat is occupied."

"Then it must be the Saturday. Oliver," I said, overwhelmed, "I . . . we, *all* of us, we won't know how to thank you for this."

"There will not be any need to thank me. I shall look upon it as a means to enable me to fulfil an obligation. There is, however, one small thing that I should mention.

"Oh," I said, "what small thing is that?"

"It is a condition," he said.

"A condition?"

"The condition is that you come back to this establishment as my second rider."

I might have expected something like this, but it had not occurred to me and now I was shocked into silence.

"You do understand, Kathryn," Oliver's cool voice said. "Quite simply, what I am saying is, no second rider, no festival of dressage."

TWENTY

"Flowers in the *manège*," Francesca said in astonishment, "live *chamber* music?"

From the tone of her voice, one might have imagined I had suggested that Oliver, as his pièce de résistance, was planning to turn himself into a frog.

I had forgotten that Francesca was not familiar with dressage, or High School, that the converted farm buildings in the Ensdale yard and the long rows of identical sectional timber boxes at the Northern Riding Centre where she had trained for her examinations, set the limits to her expectations of equestrian splendour. She had never seen the gilt-framed pier-glass mirrors in the Count's riding school, his decorative urns spilling out their extravagant flower arrangements, his tumbling pigeons, nor his fountain. She had never even allowed herself to question me about Oliver's training centre.

"Dressage is a bit like that," I tried to explain, "being a classical art it is quite compatible with flowers and chamber music and chandeliers."

"*Chandeliers?*"

"There won't actually *be* chandeliers," I said patiently, "there will be spotlights though, and the quintet will be playing Beethoven perhaps, or Verdi."

I could visualise it all as I described it, San Domingo's coat shining like glass, his plaited mane braided with ribbons to match the floral displays, cream, and gold, and crimson.

"And Oliver will receive a standing ovation, as always. People have torn up the flowers before now," I told her, "and thrown them into the arena."

Francesca frowned. With her scoop half-embedded in a sack of dried sugarbeet, she paused for a moment, as if to consider if such excessive behaviour could possibly be justified.

"And what will Oliver *do* for this solo display?" she enquired.

"*Piaffe*," I said, "*voltes* in passage, flying changes every stride, that kind of thing."

"Goodness." Even allowing for her personal prejudices, she could not help but be impressed.

I upended my bucket of water into the huge tub in which we steeped the sugarbeet overnight before feeding.

"You have never realised," I said, "how talented he is, how famous."

"No." She pondered the truth of this, allowing the grey, unappetising pulp to trickle slowly out of the scoop, watching it collect and float upon the surface of the water. "No, I suppose I never have." With typical honesty, she added, "I have never wanted to."

There was more to tell. I could have gone on to describe how, at the reception beforehand, Oliver, in the centre of *Tio Fino* dignitaries, would allow himself to be displayed in the tailcoat, wearing the white breeches with the doeskin strappings, and the long polished boots cut higher on the outside to emphasize the elegant length of leg, the unmistakable golden head shining out amongst the dark of the Spanish grandees, the shippers, their press officers and publicists as they made their way slowly from group to group. I could have continued, relating how the caballerizos who, only half an hour previously would have been putting the finishing touches to the horses, braiding the last plaits, putting on bandages, rubbing up the black, deep-seated German saddles with their straight flaps and their extended girth straps, getting ready the bridles with their long-cheeked bits and bradoons, their curbchains, and their browbands and nosebands padded with soft, white leather, would now be obliged to appear, with their hair slicked back and their fingernails scrubbed, wearing their uniform of dark blue cotton breeches, full-sleeved shirts and *Tio Fino* waistcoats, in order to hand round trays of canapes and sherry. I could also have said that they were discouraged from conversation with the public beyond the conventional responses decreed by good manners, and strictly forbidden to discuss what went on in the stables, that although their attentions were supposedly addressed to the public, they were ever watchful for Oliver's smallest movement, alert for every gesture. Amongst the decanters there would be a bottle of super-dry fino reserved solely for his consumption, and his glass would have a thread of wine-coloured cotton wound round the stem to distinguish it from the rest, so that he should not be presented, in error, with something which would offend his palate. I could have told Francesca all this, but there was something more pressing, something more important to discuss. Somehow I had to tell her that I had agreed to go back to the training centre as second rider.

For several days I had plotted and planned how I could tell her. I had even paved the way for my confession by suggesting that when she moved to Moor Park she should take on two or three capable working pupils who would work in the yard, performing all the basic tasks in return for training towards their basic examinations in riding and stable management. But Francesca had been scornful of such an arrangement.

"Have you any idea how long it takes to train anyone to be *remotely* useful in the yard?" she had demanded, "I suppose you think, like most people who have never experienced it first hand, that the working pupil system is just a way to get the stables mucked out for nothing? Don't you realise they have to be under *constant* supervision and have *hours* of instruction every day? How am I going to find time to do all that on top of the work I have to do already? And anyway," she had added with unarguable practicality, "where would they sleep?" I had not pursued the idea of the working pupils.

What I had decided was that I should open the conversation by talking about our pupils generally, leading on to the frustrations of teaching children and ponies when one's heart was really not in it, when one longed to be working with more highly trained horses, and having thus prepared her for what was to come, I would confess that I had never really enjoyed riding school work, and was seriously considering a move back to some form of higher equitation. This was how I had planned to lead up to it, feeling my way, breaking the news as gently as I could, but naturally, when the time came, I could not be patient, I had to come straight out with it.

"Francesca," I said, "I am afraid I shall be leaving in a month's time. I have to go back to Oliver."

I did not think she could have heard me at first, she looked at me in such a matter-of-fact way, continuing with what she was doing, picking up the broom handle and using it to stir the beet pulp into the water.

"I have to go back," I said, "we made a bargain."

"Well, yes," Francesca said in a calm voice. "I rather thought you might have. I expect the bargain was that Oliver would stage the Festival of Dressage if you would agree to go back to him as second rider. When you told me he had asked, I never really imagined that he would accept your refusal as final. Oliver has not got where he is by giving up easily. I knew he would find a way."

For all her ignorance of his achievements, I thought, how well she knows him. And she had expected this. She had guessed that it would happen and she had been able to live with it. I realised that Francesca, in her perspicacity, had grasped more of the situation then I had given her credit for, more even, than I had known myself, that she had seen this sort of conclusion as inevitable, and had anticipated it. I felt ashamed. I looked down into the blackening whirlpool of sugar beet.

"I won't be going back as second rider right away. I shall have to take my old job back for a while. Oliver has given John Englehart a month's notice."

This was something I had anticipated, but still it had been a shock to hear it. I did not blame Oliver for his decision, because I had known that John Englehart would not be able to continue to hold down his job, that his obsession with Oliver would hopelessly impair his efficiency, but I hoped the fact that he had told me about the sponsor's enquiry into the beating of the caballerizo had not been a contributing factor to his dismissal. I felt desperately sorry for him, knowing how much it would hurt, wondering where he would go, what he would do. I knew that my leaving Pond Cottage Riding School would not cause me a quarter as much pain, but:

"Francesca, I am *sorry*," I said.

"It's all right," she replied in a careless tone, "if you choose to allow yourself to be blackmailed by Oliver, there is not a lot I can do about it."

I had not thought of it as blackmail, or that by agreeing to go back I had exposed a weakness on my part. Rather, I had viewed it as a sacrifice made in order that St. Chad's should have a roof, St. Luke should have peace of mind, and Francesca should eventually inherit some respectable furniture. Of course, this was nonsense .

"I expect that, as usual, you have managed to convince yourself that he needs you, that he isn't just making use of your talent to further his own ends, that there is more to it than that?" Francesca's grey-green eyes regarded me levelly across the plastic tub. "If you have managed to convince yourself, if you can believe that, then good luck to you," she said.

I did not want to go into this. More than anything I wanted to believe that Oliver needed me. All the years of my life, it seemed, I had clung to this belief even though at times it had been miserably torn and tattered, and now I was reluctant to lose my last shred of hope. I was afraid to let go.

"I do know that you *want* to go back," Francesca said. "I know you haven't been happy here. And I know you love him. I can understand that. You always have. But I think you should accept that Oliver neither loves nor needs anyone. I just hope you know that Oliver is incapable of love. Oliver has never cared for anyone apart from himself. I have told you before what I think of Oliver, and my opinion hasn't changed. Oliver is obscene. Oliver is a filthy, conniving, heartless bastard."

I looked up at her in reproach, but as this had been said without enmity, as it had been stated as fact, I did not challenge it. Instead I felt relieved that she had taken everything so well, when I had half-expected a scene.

"You must promise me that you will get help," I said. "You must advertise for someone. A qualified person perhaps, someone who can help with the instruction."

Francesca removed the broom handle from the glistening sugar beet.

"Oh, I don't think I want to *pay* anyone," she said in an artless voice, "I rather thought I might take on a couple of working pupils."

★   ★   ★

Saturday morning. The usual mêlée of children, ponies and parents, the usual last-minute fussing over the length of leathers, the security of girths, the correct fitting of hat harnesses. There was even the anxiously animated presence of Davina's mother.

"I do realise she doesn't *enjoy* hacking," she confided, "in fact, she is not at *all* keen to go, but I do feel that after the most *unfortunate* incident last time, she ought to be encouraged to go out – we don't want it to become a *phobia*, do we?"

The outside telephone bell shrilled. It was a relief to

escape to the comparative sanctuary of the tack room.

"Kathryn?" It was Oliver's voice.

"Oliver?" A silence. "Oliver, are you there?"

"I am," the voice was strained, "but regretfully, I am not the bearer of very good news."

"Oliver, what is it?" My heart plummeted. "You don't mean, you *can't* mean the sponsors have changed their minds about allowing you to stage the Festival of Dressage?"

"I am afraid so."

"Oh, *Oliver* . . ."

Immediately I thought of St. Luke, reading my message, smiling in his gentle, unworldly manner, feeling the intolerable weight of his obsessive responsibility lifted from his shoulders, thanking God, lifting the telephone in order to accept the Crabtree estimate.

"But can't you influence them? Can't you beg them, threaten them, can't you *make* them change their minds? There must be *something* you can do!"

"I am afraid not." For the first time in my life I noticed hesitation in his voice and realised that there was more to come.

"Kathryn," Oliver said, "John Englehart was discovered hanging from the gallery yesterday evening."

Nothing could have prepared me for such a blow. With my spare hand I groped in an involuntary manner for a bridle hook by which to support myself. I reeled back against the wall and watched the ceiling revolve. Shock, horror, pity and revulsion swept over me in turn, leaving me faint and sickened.

"It is not possible to go into details at the present time," Oliver said, "but I thought it circumspect to warn you. The police are still here. The sponsors are involved, naturally."

"Oh," I said, "Naturally." My voice came out as a whisper.

"Kathryn, it is not solely the fact that he committed suicide," Oliver said. "It is the reasons he gave for his action. He left a note. There were also letters. He wrote letters to me, dozens of them, almost a hundred have been found. He planted them everywhere, in the house, in the office, even in my car. The whole establishment is awash with letters detailing an imaginary relationship of the most repellent nature."

It did not take any imagination at all to realise what the letters contained.

"You mean he wanted people to think . . ."

"I mean," Oliver said, "that in my life I have been guilty of many things, but now I am to be judged against something of which I am innocent, and no one is going to believe me."

"But *I* believe you, Oliver," I said desperately, "I *knew* John Englehart, I knew what he was like, I can speak for you . . ."

I had been about to involve Francesca too, but realised that her personal opinion of Oliver would put her at a serious disadvantage when called upon to defend his morals, "and I can bring St. Luke!"

"I would prefer that you did not," he said, "I do not wish anyone else to be involved in this. You will stay away, Kathryn, I would prefer it."

"But the sponsors," I cried, "*they* know you, *surely* they don't believe . . ."

"The sponsors have already informed me that they

have no alternative but to withdraw their support. This has ruined me," Oliver said.

★ ★ ★

St. Luke answered the telephone on my fifth attempt.

"St. Luke, this is Kathryn. I'm ringing to talk to you about the message I left."

There was a puzzled silence. "Message?" he said in a vague tone.

"The message. It was delivered by Mrs. Fernley. She wrote it down for you. She left it on the hall table."

"Did she really? How *very* kind," said St. Luke.

"But you didn't receive it?"

"I don't *believe* I received it." I imagined him, looking around, going through the pockets of the tweed jacket presented to him by a man who had believed that all was lost, only to be delivered in his eleventh hour.

I was so relieved. So St. Luke had not received the message. Of course he had not. What chance had one scrap of paper to be noticed amongst all the others. Why the Vicarage was choked with scraps of paper.

"Was it important," St. Luke enquired, "the message you left?"

"Not at all," I said. "It was just to tell you we had not forgotten we had promised to help raise the money, and Francesca has some news for you. She is moving to better premises. There is more land. We are going to organise a gymkhana."

"A *gymkhana*," St. Luke was impressed.

"And after that we shall have Hunter Trials. We will not be able to raise the money all at once, but even a few hundred . . ."

"A few hundred would be *splendid*," said St. Luke in a heartfelt voice. "We have already raised two hundred and sixty four pounds and thirty three pence by means of the fête. Today I was able to add over two centimetres to the barometer."

Again I had forgotten about the fête, and in the face of his good spirits, it somehow did not seem appropriate to mention Oliver's tragic predicament.

"We will come and visit you very soon," I promised, "we are very busy at the moment because of the school holidays, but we have not forgotten you. We will be in touch."

"But of course you will. You *dear* girls," said St. Luke.

TWENTY-ONE

I did as I was told. For the next two days, I stayed away, although it was unbearably painful to do so, but I could not stay away from the funeral. John Englehart had done a terrible thing, but it had been done out of the unspeakable misery of the abandoned, without any real thought of the consequences to others, I felt sure of that. I had known him well enough to realise that Oliver's heartless dismissal would have been unendurable for him, and as for the letters, well, they had been his only solace, his imaginary affair. They had been composed out of desperation, not out of spite, and I preferred to think that he had scattered them in order to be certain that Oliver would find at least some of them, so that he should know. I felt nothing but pity for him.

Oliver attended the funeral, and appropriately, it rained, although the day before had been cloudless, and there had been no hint, no forecast of rain. Two caballerizos flanked him at the service and at the graveside, the dark heads protecting the golden one. No one spoke to him, and he spoke to no one. A wreath in the shape of a horse in *passage* lay amongst the floral tributes.

As the family stood, stone-faced with grief, over the

rain-splattered coffin, we walked slowly away, across the wet, slippery grass.

"You know what they are saying about me?" he said.

"Yes," I said, "I know what they are saying. I have read the newspapers."

As usual, the horse press had been the most restrained. *Beatings Alleged After Suicide at Top Dressage Establishment* had been their headline and letters both supporting and viciously attacking Oliver had appeared in the editorial pages. The popular press had been a different matter, somehow even excerpts from the letters had appeared in print and the caballerizo paid off by the sponsors had not missed the opportunity to double his money.

"And if it were true?" he said.

"Is it true, Oliver?"

"If it were?"

"If it were true," I said, "I don't think I would be very surprised."

He turned away slightly, his eyes on a rain-washed slab set into the grass, its edges fenced with rusting fleur-de-lis.

"You always said what you thought, Kathryn. You never prevaricated."

The sight of him standing there, his good, navy coat hanging loose about his shoulders, his golden hair wet, suddenly caved in my heart completely.

"Oliver . . ." I began, and I was going to say, whatever you have done, however you have behaved, it doesn't matter, you only have to ask, you only have to tell me you need me. I will come with you, wherever you choose to go, but I did not say it because unexpectedly, terrifyingly, he dropped his head into his hands.

"You do know," he said in an agonised voice, "that they have taken San Domingo."

I did not know. I could not take it in at first. I could not believe it. I knew the sponsors had not been without sympathy for him, the publicity department had almost been prepared to ride out the storm, but the board of directors with due regard to the sensibilities of their shareholders, had been forced to recommend that the sponsorship be withdrawn with the greatest possible speed and the establishment had already been advertised for sale. To remove the sponsorship, to strip Oliver of the trappings that his talent, his fame and his glamour had earned him was terrible – yet somehow, in the light of all that had happened, understandable; but to take away his beloved San Domingo – only I perhaps, fully realised what this would mean to him.

I stood beside him in the bleak churchyard, on turf impregnated with the tears of centuries, and I was helpless with the utter wretchedness of it all. I wanted to throw my arms around his bowed shoulders, to tell him I loved him still, that I had never stopped loving him, but I no longer knew how. I was afraid to touch him. I was paralysed, useless. He was beyond comfort and I was hopeless with the knowledge that not a single thing I could say or do would bring him relief.

I do not know how long we stood there, but long enough for him to recover his composure, to take a deep, uneven breath, to raise his head, to present me with a face in which there was enough of the Oliver I knew to challenge me to notice that the eyelashes were wet. Then he turned, motioned to the waiting caballerizos to follow him, and walked away.

* * *

When I returned to Pond Cottage several hours later, Francesca was waiting for me in the yard. "Well?" she demanded. "What will he do? Where will he go? Has he decided?"

"I have no idea," I said, "I didn't even ask."

"You didn't *ask!*" Francesca stared at me. She was wearing the inevitable begrimed jodhpurs and her anorak with the collar turned up against the rain, but her head was bare, and the curls of hair escaping from her plait dripped beads of water.

"You didn't ASK?"

I knew it must sound stupid, but Francesca had not been there. She did not realise how impossible it had been.

"I couldn't ask. I could hardly speak to him. I wish you could have seen," I said, biting my lip, "how destroyed he was."

"He must not be destroyed," Francesca said firmly.

"Oh, *Francesca*," I leaned against the stable wall, feeling unutterably anguished and exhausted by it all, "how can you possibly say that? You, who have been his sternest critic."

"That may be true. It is true," Francesca decided, "but I have been thinking, and I have been looking at the newspapers, and I have come to the conclusion that Oliver has been unjustly treated. He has been infamously slandered. He didn't *kill* John Englehart, he isn't a murderer, and all of these things they accuse him of, none of them are *proven*."

"No," I agreed, "but some of them are true nevertheless."

"*Kathryn*, do you want to *help* Oliver, or not?"

I put my hands up to my face in despair.

"Of course I want to help him! I want to help him more than I have ever wanted anything in the whole of my life! If you really want to know, I would cry and scream to heaven. I would *die* if I thought it would help him, but I know that it would not. It is all futile. Nothing can help him."

"Oh yes it can," Francesca said. The grey-green eyes regarded me in a purposeful manner. "Oh yes it *can*."

"What can?" I looked at her in disbelief. "Who can?" Only if the world can be persuaded to slip back in time can Oliver be helped now, I thought, and even Francesca in her present mood of determination, would be hard-pressed to arrange that.

"Tell me first what you think he will do," she said. "You must have some idea. You know him better than anybody."

"Untrue," I said, "But a common mistake." With the back of my sodden glove I wiped an irritating trickle of rain from my cheek. "I should think he may very well go abroad. It seems to me to be the only thing he can do."

"Oh no," she said decidedly, "we must not let him do that."

"We?" I looked at her questioningly, and with slight exasperation. "Francesca, I don't think he actually has a choice. I think he *has* to leave."

"Going abroad won't help him," Francesca said. "I don't know anything about dressage, but I do know that at the very top, any international sport is very tightly knit. Everyone will know who he is and speculation will sometimes be worse than fact. It will be no easier for him abroad, it will be even more difficult. He will be amongst strangers in a foreign country, he will be lonely. Remember," she added darkly, "what happened to Oscar Wilde."

I would have laughed at the comparison if I had the heart for it. "I think I would prefer not to think about Oscar Wilde," I said.

"Well I think that Oliver should stay," Francesca declared. "I think he should take everything they can throw at him, I think he should endure it and show them he is not to be defeated, and start again. His reputation may be in shreds," she acknowledged, "but he still has his talent, nobody can take that away from him, nobody can deny that he is the very best."

It all sounded very fine, very noble, put like that, but:

"How *can* he start again," I said despairingly, "what with? Oliver owns nothing, he has nothing. They have even taken San Domingo away from him. He has no horses, no money, and nowhere to go."

"Oh, but he has," Francesca said, a note of triumph in her voice, "he can have Moor Park Stables."

"*Moor Park Stables?*"

"And why not?" she demanded, "The stables are good, there is land, there is a flat. He can take liveries, give lessons, what more could he want? Why on earth shouldn't he have Moor Park Stables? Give me one good reason why not?"

"Because you are going to move there," I said, "because you need them, and you deserve them, that's why not."

"That isn't a good enough reason."

We stood in the rain, in the appallingly decrepit stable yard, with the mud forming around us again even as we stood, and I looked at Francesca in wonder and disbelief. I did not understand how she could be prepared to forsake all that was promised, the convenience, the order, the comfort, the peace of mind, for the hideous uncertainty, the chaos, the dreadful discomfort of what she had until now so cheerfully endured. I thought there must be some defect in her nature which compelled her away from the easy path, towards one littered with rocks and beset with brambles. It was quite beyond my comprehension. I could not believe that she had thought to consider it. It seemed impossible that she could have suggested it.

"You can't mean it? You couldn't, you *wouldn't* let Oliver have Moor Park Stables, whilst you stayed on *here*?"

"Oh but I could, you see," she said, "I can do it easily. And Simon will agree, I'm sure. And if he doesn't like the idea at first, well," she lifted her dripping shoulders slightly, "there are always ways and means you know, of persuading people to do things."

A sentiment with which Oliver might have agreed. I looked at her sharply. She was perfectly resolute.

"I shall *do* it," she said. "I am quite determined. Oliver may be a swine and a bastard, he may have done loathsome things, but you have to let me help him now, if I can. You have to allow it."

"It is not up to me to allow or disallow anything," I said, "I am just at a loss to understand why you would do it."

"I would have thought that you, would have understood that quite well."

She turned her head slightly and brushed irritably at the tendrils of hair plastered to her brow. I thought her eyes had filled with tears, but then again, it could have been the rain.

"Do not imagine," she said, in a stiff little voice, "that you were the only one of us to love Oliver, because there was a time when I loved him more than anybody."

TWENTY-TWO

We rode to Oliver. There was really no other way. Across country it was not so far, about nine miles. An unexplained, unspoken sense of urgency hastened our progess.

Across Moor Park we cantered, passing the rows of empty loose boxes without a glance, and along the bridleway where we slowed our impatient horses to a trot. Their hooves made hollow, watery sounds on the tarmac. Over the river bridge we trotted, where below us the yellowish water swirled and raced as the surrounding land drained into it. Cutting through another bridleway, where untrimmed hedges snagged at our clothing, we traversed a deep and sticky headland into which the horses sank to their hocks where the plough had claimed every inch. Labouring now, we progressed by means of roads and verges until finally we arrived at the end of the immaculate drive where a cluster of 'For Sale' notices brutally offended the eye.

In the silent, empty stable yard, not even the ghost of a horse, remained. Only the youngest of the caballerizos was to be found, sitting sheltered from the rain beneath the dripping overhang, waiting it seemed, for something, for somebody. He appeared to believe we had come to persuade him to leave and held out his hands, palms foremost, as if he would push us away, although we had not even dismounted from the horses.

"I not leave him," he said. "I never leave him. Never. I stay here. I wait." He was perfectly firm, totally adamant.

"Where is he?" Francesca demanded. "We must see him. It's important."

He shrugged. "He not tell me. He go walking. He tell me stay here, he come back soon. I wait. I never leave him," he reiterated, "never." He sat tight on his bale of straw and looked at us defiantly. He was as immovable as the Rock of Gibraltar.

"Walking?" Francesca looked across at me. "In this weather?"

"He has coat," the caballerizo assured us, "he has good coat."

"He has good coat already soaked through," I said, and was seized by panic. "Francesca, he wouldn't . . . ."

"I don't know," she said. But she had wrenched the chesnut's steaming head round and was away down the drive at a gallop before I could collect my wits. The roan cob swerved after her, flying along the gravel out of my control. For a moment I was reminded of my first ride on Simpson at Bickerton Show, all those years ago. That ride, also, had been for Oliver.

At the end of the drive, Francesca slowed up, unsure of which direction to take. I knew the country. As we crashed out onto the road I led the way to the river. I made first for the bridge, spotted a field leading down to the bank, and set the roan cob galloping alongside the flow. Miles and miles we seemed to ride, plunging through the floods, skirting minor bridges across the lanes, bypassing, sometimes trespassing across private property, scanning the fields for tractor crossings by which to negotiate minor rivulets racing to join the main flow. But we found what we were looking for at last, face downwards in the little watershed before the thundering weir, in front of the grating amidst the accumulated rubbish collected by the river on its never ending journey; the cans, the bottles, the cartons, the plastic bags, the remnants of things once desired, but soon exhausted and cast away.

Together, we managed to get him out of the water. We laid him carefully on the bank. We straightened and tidied his clothing, smoothed the thin silk shirt, arranged his black tie. We buttoned his good navy coat. Amongst the bobbing refuse, we found his missing shoe and forced it onto his unwilling foot. I combed his golden hair with my fingers as best I could. He was quite cold. By mute and mutual agreement, we made no attempt at resuscitation. It had been his decision, he had always decided for himself, after all, and neither of us would have cared to face him had we succeeded.

I did not weep. He had always detested any display of emotion and this knowledge helped me to hang onto my self-control. Francesca, too, cheated of her great sacrifice, consigned to a life of order and relative comfort, did not weep either.

Only when he was composed to our satisfaction did we call an ambulance. Francesca set out silently on the exhausted chestnut gelding to find a telephone, and I sat on the bank, holding onto the roan cob's reins to foil his determined efforts to follow, watching the rain collect, like tears, in Oliver's beautiful blue eyes.

EPILOGUE

I came today, Oliver, to say goodbye. I could not do it yesterday, there were too many people. We did not expect a lot. We thought, things being as they were, it would be a rather quiet affair. We should have known, shouldn't we, we should have realised you would still draw the crowds, but we were simply overwhelmed by the numbers. The Vicarage and the garden were packed with people, and as usual, we were improvident; we even ran out of teabags. Francesca had to run down to the village shop. Not long afterwards we ran out of food; there was nothing left in the house with which to fill a sandwich, not even a sliver of cucumber. How you would have loathed it. How angry you would have been. We could never do anything to your complete satisfaction, could we Oliver? Well, rest assured that yesterday we failed you again.

One thing we did not run out of was sherry. Boxes and boxes of it were delivered by lorry – we had to put it in the greenhouse. All of the *Tio Fino* people came. I expect you find that wry. They have given me San Domingo, they said you had told them I had the potential to make an Olympic standard dressage rider, but I shall not even try.

Count Von Der Drehler is going to buy him, and the proceeds will go to buy St. Chad's a new roof. That way I shall have fulfilled on your behalf, the last of your obligations. I feel you would approve of this, but possibly not of the next part. With the money I have left, I am going into partnership with Sandy Headman. He and I have arranged to sub-let six loose boxes from Francesca at Moor Park. I shall break and school young horses and he will show hunters in the summer, and in the winter will take hunter liveries. Who knows, sometime in the future I might train a dressage horse of my own.

Yesterday was the most appalling ordeal. We would have liked the service to have been in St. Chad's, but there would not have been room. As it was, St. Aidan's was tightly packed, and many more stood outside. Charity Ensdale, and the little caballerizo who waited were both removed from the service. Francesca's beautiful face was like a stone. St. Luke wept. In all these years I have never seen St. Luke shed a tear, but he wept, quite openly, throughout the service. There were so many tears, Oliver, so many tears. But not from me. I won't cry for you. I can't.

This is a bloody, bloody thing that you have done, Oliver. It should never have ended like this, never. I don't know if you are listening, you never listened before, and now you have the perfect excuse for not hearing, but I honestly do not know how you could have done this to me.

I looked everywhere for your message, for your goodbye. I searched the house, the stables, the car, even the commentary box, for some word, for something to prove you thought of me, of how I might feel. You could have left me something, it would not have taken a minute of your time, but there was nothing. Nothing at all. Francesca was right; you were a bastard.